D O P P E L **GAN** G **E R**

DOPPELGANGER

□

□

A NOVEL BY

ERIC HIGGS

ST. MARTIN'S PRESS

NEW YORK

□

Design by John Fontana

Library of Congress Cataloging in Publication Data

Higgs, Eric. C.
    Doppelganger.

    I. Title.
PS3558.I3623D6   1987   813'.54   86-26158
ISBN 0-312-00121-5

First Edition

10 9 8 7 6 5 4 3 2 1

For Paul Liepa, my editor

"What the inner voice says will not disappoint the hoping soul."

—VON SCHILLER

ACKNOWLEDGMENTS

Many thanks to Mitch Nauffts, Harry Trumbore and Robin Rue, for performance above and beyond the call of duty.

O N E

The shove sent Mr. Sam tripping backward, arms flailing wildly. His ankles hit against the service island's curb and he started going down, right between the pumps for unleaded and unleaded supreme. His hands scrabbled desperately for anything that might break his fall, and his heart leapt when he latched onto a thick rubber hose. But as soon as it drew tight, the nozzle clattered free of the boot.

The old man hit the concrete with a painful grunt.

Marvin Moy advanced on him quickly, fists balled, head

lowered. He told himself this had been a long time coming. Hell, *more* than a long time coming. This had been brewing since the first day, from the very first time Mr. Sam had stuck his gnarled finger against Marvin's chest and told him that he was a *fuckpoke* this and a *fuckpoke* that, and there wasn't a *queerboy shitstick* under God's blue sky that didn't have more *toad puke* between the ears than *Marvin fucking Moy!* But now all the yappa-ta-yap was done, wasn't it? Now Mr. Sam had taken things a little too far, hadn't he? Now he'd poked his finger a little too hard, leaned his bad breath a little too close, until all a man could do was just shove the old bastard away, giving it enough mustard to send him tumbling into the pumps.

Marvin hopped to the island and paused, flanked by the squat pumps. Mr. Sam was trying to push himself upright, awkward as an upended turtle, the deep lines of his face contorted with an old man's surprise and pain. Marvin's lungs worked like a bellows, making the furnace in his belly glow white-hot. There were a thousand things he'd always wanted to do to the old shit, and now that the time had come, he decided on something that would be just slow enough to make it last a little bit, something that would be savage and poetical at the same time.

Marvin flipped the unleaded's reset lever, and the money and gallon totalizers whirred and clicked back to zero.

He stepped off the island and dropped his knee onto Mr. Sam's chest. The air came out of the old man's lungs in an explosive gasp. Marvin used one big hand to clamp down on Mr. Sam's leathery throat, the other to grab the nozzle lying nearby. Mr. Sam kicked and fought and tried to wrestle himself free, but the hand on his throat felt as cold and hard as Alabama marble. Marvin jammed the spout against the old man's lips, and after a moment's resistance, the dentures gave and slipped sideways. The nozzle suddenly went deep, pressing against the softness of tongue.

Marvin narrowed his eyes. The nozzle's trigger was greasily cold. "Think I'm a fuckpoke now?" His teeth were clenched tight, the words coming out in a whisper. "Eh, Mr. Sam? Think I'm a goddamn faggot fuckpoke now? Eh? *Eh?*"

Rich fumes wafted upward. The old man gagged convulsively, rivulets of fuel pouring down either side of his mouth. Marvin pressed down with his full weight, holding Mr. Sam fast to the concrete. He squeezed the trigger to its stops.

"Whoa, whoa, hold steady, Mr. Sam." The puddle of gasoline around the old man's head grew bigger, but most of the fuel seemed to be going where it was directed. Yes indeed. Most every goddamn drop. "Hold steady while I fill 'er the fuck up. Yeah, there we go, you old son of a bitch. Yes, sir . . ."

It was white, but stiff and papery like a great sheet of milky plastic. Then the sense of it suddenly hit him, and he knew that it was just a sail, a *big* damn sail but just a sail, thank Christ, and he was out here with a job to do, one that he had to do quick. The jib was out of control, billowing outward and then slapping back, popping and snapping against the aluminum mast, sounding like a string of firecrackers. The deck of the small boat was slick and wobbly, and Marvin kept one arm locked around the mast as he tried to rein it in. He caught a piece of the stiff Dacron but the wind gusted and snatched it away. Marvin nearly slipped, but he wrapped both arms around the mast and held on, and then the wind shifted and the sail suddenly came back, wrapping itself around him, and he fought to contain the panic that told him the thing had taken on a

3

life of its own, that it was intent on wrenching him free of the mast and casting him into the freezing ocean, and just as the scream started to well up from his throat he penetrated through into consciousness and sat upright in bed, eyes wide in the darkness, sweat damp against his forehead, the only sound in the room the deep, rapid gasping of his own breath.

He swung his feet to the floor and padded toward the bathroom. He knocked over a chair and fell to his knee, but quickly pushed himself up and kept going, rushing now, as if getting to the bathroom was the most important thing in the world. He went straight to the sink, turned the handle on the cold water spigot, and started splashing water on his face, the fastest way he knew to distance himself from the dream.

And that's all it was—just a goddamn dream. Nothing to get upset about. Keep remembering what that doctor lady in the advice column said: Sometimes your dreams are little tricks your subconscious plays. *Keep thinking of it as a little trick, and you'll be okay.*

Marvin turned off the spigot. His heart had slowed to its normal muscular thud. He took a towel from the rack and dried his face carefully. The darkened shapes in the tiny bathroom became familiar and comforting.

Then he sank to the rim of the chipped bathtub, biting down on the wad of towel in his mouth, straining so hard that the cords on his neck began to cramp.

But, doctor lady, what do you do if you wake up every living day wondering if you're losing your mind?

Marvin stepped onto the balcony of the two-story garage/apartment, clad in his jogging attire. Sometimes exercise helped clear things up. Sometimes not. But it was always worth a try.

4

He went down the wooden stairway carefully, mindful of the risers slick with dew. Although dawn was at hand, the fog kept everything dark as midnight. It was so thick this morning that Marvin could barely make out the dim bulk of the Victorian mansion only thirty yards away. The mansion had been subdivided into small apartments years ago, and Marvin lived in the property's only detached building. For some lost reason the complex had been dubbed the Cota Arms.

The staircase faced the mansion's small backyard, the centerpiece of which was a fountain long since run dry. A concrete Aphrodite stood in the bowl's center, the vase in her hands tipped to no purpose. Marvin worked the latch on the wooden gate and stepped through an arched trellis of bougainvillea. He went into the alley that bisected the block, originally designed as access to the rear garages of what had been, in the 1920s, an upper-middle-class neighborhood. He raised his hands high, then slowly stretched down so that his palms rested flat against the cracked pavement. He repeated this twice more, breathing deeply of the moist air.

He paused before beginning his jog, looking at the dark shapes of his big hands. He thought about the dream with Mr. Sam in it, about its violence and savagery, so different from real life, where even verbal confrontation made him physically ill.

Marvin shook his head and began jogging. He reached the end of the alley and looked both ways before crossing the street. There was another alley on the other side, and although it was unlit, Marvin knew the way well. The jumble of closely set houses and apartments was as lifeless as the previous block. The distant boom of the surf grew louder.

Mr. Sam might not be the most easygoing boss in the world, Marvin thought, but he'd never wanted to strike him, never even *thought* about it. Tell him to shove his lousy job, maybe. But to hold him down and jam a gas nozzle—

Marvin jogged faster, telling himself there was no sense in blaming Mr. Sam for his own bad luck, or bad planning, or whatever it was you called it that made you a pump jockey at a run-down filling station for two years, with no prospects of things ever getting better.

He paused at one of the cross-streets, jogging in place while a police cruiser went by slowly, the fog making its headlight beams as defined as a spaceship's death rays. Marvin saw a lone silhouette inside, glancing his way. Marvin waved. The white sedan continued on its way.

He crossed the street and began building up speed, preparing to jump over the low concrete wall that demarked the beach, but slowed down when something skittered behind a big trash can, catching his eye. Marvin stopped and looked, then smiled. He knelt, extending a hand.

"Kitty, kitty?" Marvin was breathing hard, but tried to keep his voice to a singsong cadence. "Hey, kitty cat?"

Much to his surprise, the cat heeded his summons. It poked its head out, peering around the side of the can.

Marvin's smile grew bigger. "Hello, kitty. Hello, fella."

The cat let out a rusty meow and hobbled into view. Its right forepaw was mangled and splotched with caked blood, forcing it to move in a kind of grotesque hop. Marvin's heart clenched with pity.

"Aw, kitty . . ." Marvin reached out and scratched its nicked, torn ears. It was a battle-scarred tom, mostly black but with some patches of white. "Poor kitty. Poor old pussy cat."

The cat closed its eyes and was soon giving out a little drumroll of a purr. It relaxed enough to let its wounded paw touch the sidewalk, then quickly lifted it up.

Marvin reached to pick it up and stroke it, but as soon

6

as he put his hand on its back it came alive with anger and scratched at him, then backed off, hissing.

Marvin yelped and stood up, cupping his scratched hand. The cat scrabbled to its hiding place behind the trash can, and for a moment Marvin felt like pushing the can on its side and giving the cat a kick that would surely end its misery.

But he checked himself and stepped over the low wall onto the beach instead. He began jogging through the powdery sand, shaking his scratched hand. He was going to have to drench it in peroxide when he got back to his apartment, that was for sure.

Stupid fucking cat, he thought. If he had really wanted to be a Good Samaritan—never mind the scratch—he should've stomped the cat out of its misery. It was obviously going to starve in a few days anyway. Why not go ahead and—

Marvin lowered his head and concentrated on running. The barest hint of dawn lightened the fog to a battleship-gray. The breakers were barely visible, the white foam pale and faded. Marvin reached the smooth, hardpacked sand at the water's edge and started running parallel to the surf line.

The waves crashed against the sand in an irregular jumble of flat, rolling booms, interspersed with occasional bits of silence. Marvin jogged for half a mile, his mind slewing back to the cat. Maybe stomping it would've been too harsh. Having it put to sleep by a vet would be kinder. But what business of it was his anyway? Thousands of stray cats died every day.

He picked up his pace. The dark shape of beached seaweed appeared suddenly, and without thinking he took it with a long jump. He went faster. The rocky outline of a basalt jetty loomed ahead, and he barely slowed as he approached it. He scampered up the boulders with practiced ease, hopping from one foothold to the next, keeping his speed up. He reached the top and jumped, and hit the hard sand with a grunt. He immediately began rushing forward, his legs pumping like a lineman's at the snap.

He accelerated rapidly, feeding on a reservoir of energy. Soon he was in a flat-out sprint, arms and legs lifting high. The damp air streamed in and out of his open mouth. His feet pounded against the sand. He reached the point where he was holding nothing back, where arms and legs were working at maximum efficiency, and still it seemed as if his energy had been barely tapped, that he could continue accelerating indefinitely. He ran without thought to pacing or endurance, only in blind submission to the explosion of the sprint.

Marvin suddenly felt as if he had climbed to the apex of his trajectory—like a jet fighter at the apogee of a steep climb, giving its occupant a prolonged moment of weightlessness. The energy left him, turning his limbs into loose weights of fleshy muscle. He tired, legs stiffening so that they hit the sand flat-footed. He slowed to a wide-gaited walk, hands on hips, air whistling into his lungs. A stream of spit went out and snicked back against his chin. He wiped it away.

He walked until his breathing was under control. He couldn't see more than fifty yards in any direction, but there was just enough light to make the sand a pale beige, the ocean a roiling gray. He stopped and bent down, hacking out a wad of phlegm. The long muscles in his legs began to stiffen, and he started walking again.

Marvin found himself thinking that the thing to do would be to take the cat to a vet and have him fix the paw. How much would it cost, anyway? Five bucks? Ten? He could certainly spare that. There was better than two hundred in his checking account, not counting what was needed for next month's rent.

The sweat was beginning to chill against his forehead. So what if there was a no-pets clause at the Cota Arms? Screw 'em. An old tom like that deserved to spend its last years on a cozy windowsill, drowsing in the sun and meowing hello when Marvin came home from work, watching with intense interest as Marvin poured a bowl of Purina Cat Chow, sitting in his lap while Marvin worked on his drawings. . . .

Sure. Why not? No one would know about it—the manager had never *been* in his apartment. In fact, he'd never had a visitor of any sort. Marvin allowed himself a rueful smile. Who'd notice a cat?

The fog had lost its thick tendrils and was now more of a flat, even haze. Just ahead was the long outline of another jetty, the one that protected the entrance to Mission Bay. He turned around and began jogging back. He looked at the footprints he'd made on the jog up and brought his knees higher, making his stride longer. He made a deal with himself. If he could run flat-out all the way back to the municipal pier, he'd reward himself with a half-dozen-donut breakfast from Winchell's. And a carton of icy-cold milk. He would go to Winchell's with the cat tucked under his arm. Yeah. His new pal.

He brought himself to the verge of a sprint, focusing on the hard sand immediately in front of him, and the driftwood and clumps of seaweed went by quickly.

Marvin closed on the stone jetty rapidly. The fog made it seem more distant than it actually was, and he was upon it before he was ready. He tried to plant his foot on the first boulder, hoping that momentum would carry him past any momentary imbalance and onto the next foothold. But his foot slipped sideways, and Marvin's knee struck stone.

A ferocious bolt of pain shot through his leg. He cried out and fell backward onto the hardpacked sand. He rolled, hands clasped tightly to his knee. Broken, he thought. Son of a bitch is busted up into a thousand pieces. The waves of pain mixed with a great, roiling nausea, and he whimpered as he twisted in the sand.

The pain finally subsided after long minutes, and Marvin managed to get himself upright. He felt sickly and frail, but when he tested his bruised knee he found it could take his weight. He began limping through the sand, parallel to the jetty, heading back toward town. Dawn had come and gone, and the early morning light was fully upon the community of Ocean Beach.

He began taking bigger strides through the powdery sand, angling toward the low wall where he'd first crossed onto the beach, and the stiffness in his knee began to loosen. He stepped over the wall and looked up and down the sidewalk. Nothing, save the battered trash cans lined up in an uneven row.

"Kitty?" he called. "Kitty, kitty?"

He walked over to the nearest trash can. It was a freshly painted fifty-gallon drum, with a yellow sticker below the rim that read TAN . . . *don't litter*/COPPERTONE. The old tom might still be hiding behind it.

Marvin grabbed the rim and rolled it a little ways from the wall, half expecting the cat to come skittering out from behind. Then something inside the can caught his eye.

The tom was lying at the bottom, utterly limp, its little pink tongue lolling out of his mouth.

Its head had been wrenched halfway around.

T W O

Mr. Samuel R. Hattstaedt slipped his key in the lock at precisely 6:05. He went into the service station's office and turned on the overheads, then snubbed out his Salem 100 in the aluminum ashtray. He opened the side door and went into the service bays, flicking on the big fluorescents. He hated to waste electricity, but it looked like this goddamn fog was going to keep things on the dark side for at least another hour. And that fuckpoke weatherman on last night's news had worn his toothiest Jewboy grin when he said the forecast was picture-postcard pretty.

Yeah, Jack. Sure thing. Maybe you'd like to kick in a little something for my utility bills.

Mr. Sam opened the first of the three big rollup doors to the service bays, pulling on the steel chain that made the slatted aluminum clatter upward. Then he opened the other two doors, the concrete walls echoing with a series of racketing bangs. There were two cars inside, a little Toyota Celica in for some tranny work, thank Christ, and a shitbox Triumph Spitfire for a tune-and-lube.

That done, he went around to the side of the building to open up the restrooms. He attended to this little chore with a grim set to his mouth. Always had, ever since the day eight years ago when the morning's inspection of the ladies' room had yielded a bloody human fetus. But this morning everything looked jake, and there was even enough goop in the soap dispensers to last the day. Mr. Sam paused only long enough to spit bile into the gent's can before walking out.

He went back to the office and flicked on the switches for the service islands—three pumps at the full-serve, three at the self-serve, one at the diesel-only island. Then he unlocked the cash register, withdrew a plastic drawer with fifty bucks' worth of bills and silver, and went to the full-serve island to put it into the cashbox bolted to the steel column. He unlocked the box, took out the credit card machine and put it on top, and locked the cash drawer inside. Though the official 6:45 opening time was still a good thirty minutes off, Hattstaedt's Sup'r Serv was ready to go.

Mr. Sam went to the vending machines outside the office and dropped a quarter in the coffee machine. He pressed the button marked Light With Sugar, and when the paper cup fell into place he held in the buttons for Extra Dairy

12

Substitute and Sugar. The shit from the machine needed all the extra glop it could get. He took the cup and blew away the steam, sipped. Grimaced.

He went back inside the office and picked the San Diego *Union* off the floor, which gave him his customary twinge of satisfaction, for it was daily testament to his wiliness in business affairs. Having the paper delivered to the station meant it could be written off as a business expense— ostensibly for the customers waiting out repair jobs in the "lounge," as he was more than eager to explain to any auditor who might care to know. Not that any of the idiots waiting out a repair had enough time to look at the headlines, since they were usually too damn busy looking over a man's shoulder and telling him how to do his job.

Mr. Sam plopped his wiry frame into the swivel chair and lit up a fresh Salem. He leafed through the paper, glancing at the headlines. His hands were long and bony, mottled with ugly patches of tight pinkish skin—burn scars, acquired in 1957, souvenirs of his unsuccessful attempt to drag his wife and daughter from a burning Hudson Hornet.

Some of the men who had worked for Mr. Sam claimed he had been born mean, which was not far from wrong. Sloat, Mississippi, was a mean place to be born. Disputes tended to be settled by a close-range burst of double-ought buck, and the only men who wore coats and ties were visitors from the Bureau of Alcohol, Tobacco, and Firearms.

But Mr. Sam was not born through-and-through mean. No, that had taken some careful tending and nuturing. His stepfather had been his first great influence, a short, skinny man with watchful eyes. He was rarely given to conversations longer than one or two words, except when he was drunk. Then the watchful eyes would change to something else, to something sullen and mean-spirited, and he would tell his wife's son that life was unfair, that no matter how

13

hard a man slave-drived himself he would wind up with shit pie, and, his voice growing louder and his face turning red, he would shout that it was a world where the *big ate the little* and it was something he'd better learn *right soon.* At this point the boy's fear would take over and he would bolt and try to get away, even though he knew it would only make it worse, and the man would always catch him, an old leather shaving strop dangling from his hand, and with a voice rich with the fumes of corn liquor yell, *Now,* by God and Sonny Jesus, *now you'll learn!*

But even after childhood there was still much on the agenda in the making of the man. The Army called him up in 1951. The only thing about it that surprised him was how the other boys in his company moaned and bellyached about Basic being so tough. Sam Hattestaedt had to wonder what was so tough about getting up at four-thirty. Or shooting straight with a rifle. Or marching around in the hot sun for hours at a stretch. It wasn't tough. It was *easy.* In fact, when he became the first man in his company to sew on a corporal's stripes, he could begin to see the lifer's viewpoint, that putting in your twenty and getting a decent retirement was a hell of a lot better than what he had waiting for him back in Sloat.

His regiment was shipped to Korea shortly thereafter, and they saw action right away. But it was minor skirmishing, something that only served to liven up the long march deep into the countryside, into the barren wasteland of cold hills and deserted villages. Corporal Hattstaedt had just about decided that this war business wasn't so tough either, but then the frozen hills came alive with Chinese regulars, cutting his company off. The Americans dug in frantically and prepared for the assault, using tactics not much different than those of Custer at Little Bighorn.

But the enemy did not charge, at least not right away. First they softened the Americans up, even though they had no artillery at their disposal. What they used was something that came to be called pyschological warfare. Great bullhorns broadcast bloodthirsty messages of doom. The Americans answered with gusto. But then the Chinese turned to the few American prisoners they'd taken.

The screams were sharp and piercing in the cold night. Some of the Americans wanted to charge, but the officers held them back. Then GIs started firing in the direction of the screams, trying to put a merciful end to it. But the sites of torture were too well-protected, and the practitioners very adept at their dreadful art. The victims lasted a long, long time.

Mr. Sam crawled deep into his foxhole that night and held his carbine tight. He knew one of the prisoners, another corporal by the name of Jack Embry. He was a Louisiana fellow, real good at five-card stud. He tried stuffing frozen dirt in his ears, but even that wouldn't block it out. Nothing blocked it out—he sat there all night listening to the number of screaming voices decrease one by one. When it was finally done the Chinese started beating drums and blowing trumpets, building the cacaphony to a fearsome crescendo as they worked themselves up, finally letting out their own screams of rage as they poured down from the hills, bayonets flashing in the cold moonlight.

Mr. Sam had been fairly successful in blocking out what happened after that, keeping it in a far corner of his mind. The only thing he wanted to remember was that he had survived, and whatever he decided to do with the rest of his life (and it wasn't soldiering, that was for goddamn sure), it would be a cakewalk, for he had already been through the worst.

But he was wrong. Three years after his hitch was done, a teenage drunk slammed into the aging Hudson Hornet, knocking it from the road in a sideways roll. Mr. Sam was thrown clear. His seventeen-year-old wife and baby daughter weren't so fortunate. They were trapped inside, and by the time Mr. Sam picked himself up and hobbled back toward the wreckage, the car had become a steel furnace.

It had happened on the outskirts of a pissant little town in Texas called Salt Flat. Mr. Sam and his family had been heading for California, land of clear skies and fresh starts. But there didn't seem much point to it after the accident. Mr. Sam ended up drifting west anyway, from one minimum-wage job to the next, a thousand half-eaten meals in as many greasy spoons.

It was a journey that ended up taking two years. The highlight was a stretch of work at an all-night service station in Globe, Arizona, where the mildest and meekest looking little man he had ever seen gut-shot him with a twenty-two. That had cost Mr. Sam a couple of feet of small intestine, and a little something more. As Mr. Sam lay on the operating table thinking of the way that little fuckpoke had *smiled* as he squeezed the trigger, well . . . the doctors might as well have taken out his last dram of kindness as well, for by the time he finally thumbed his way out of Globe there was certainly none left.

Mr. Sam drained the last sweetly bitter drops of coffee. He took another drag off the butt. Almost opening time. He folded the newspaper and tossed it on his untidy desk. Then he went outside, hitching up his gray work pants, cigarette dangling from the corner of his mouth.

A battered Datsun B-210 rounded the corner and wheezed onto the station's asphalt. Well, well, well, Mr. Sam thought. If it ain't Marvin Moy the Wonder Boy in his niggermobile.

He watched the junker until it disappeared from sight, heading toward the parking slot in back of the station. The engine dieseled for a moment, then coughed and died. He heard the slam of the door. Then Marvin came walking around front, nodding hello to his boss.

Mr. Sam watched the boy's approach sourly. How a kid built like Marvin could be such a dishrag was a constant source of confusion and anger to Mr. Sam. Hell, if *he* had that same yard's worth of shoulders he'd take zero crap from no one. But not old Marv. No, sir. He acted more like a fairy college professor than a man built better than most middleweights. He just threw it away with both hands. Shit, the boy didn't even *have* to fight anybody—all he had to do was stand his ground and nine men out of ten would back down.

But then, Mr. Sam thought, some people are just born with a big black stamp on their forehead that says *loser*. Why, the boy had even admitted that he'd been booted out of the Navy with a dishonorable discharge. Now if that wasn't the sign of a fuckpoke, what was?

"Morning, Mr. Sam."

He took the Salem out and spat on the concrete. "Yeah. I want you to get started hosing down these aprons. Anything don't come right up I want you on your fuckpoke knees scrubbing it off. Then go ahead and get the tire and oil display racks out where they belong. Give the pumps a good wipedown. I'm going in to finish that tune on the Triumph, so you take all the trade until I get done."

"Sure thing, boss."

Mr. Sam took another drag off the almost-gone butt, eyes locked onto Marvin's. After a moment the boy looked down. Mr. Sam went off to the service bays, feeling a small glow of satisfaction. He often wondered exactly what it was that had got old Marv kicked out of the service. Probably got caught for swinging on some guy's crank, he thought with a thin little smile.

The first car came in just as the last of the fog was burning off, a blue Mazda GLC. It nosed into the self-serves, and by the time Marvin had finished rolling out the tire rack and had the cashbox unlocked, the bearded driver was waiting for Marvin to make change. The sale was for eight even, and while Marvin broke the man's twenty a big Olds Cutlass Supreme eased over the air line that made the service bell ding.

The Cutlass stopped by the premium full-serve. Marvin walked over as the power window rolled down, and the nice-looking middle-aged lady asked for a fill-up. He walked around the rear of the car toward the pumps, checking for things that had become second nature—worn or underinflated tires, missing valve caps, broken lenses, damaged tail pipes. He got the nozzle in and set the regulator clip on automatic, then did a quick wipedown on the rear window. He walked toward the front, going along the car's right side. Mr. Sam had told him never to use the left side—the customer might stop you to ask some dumb question, thus delaying your inspection for further possible sales items. He hit the windshield and checked the blades, which were marginal, and just as he was going into the under-the-hood routine he saw an elderly white MGB pull into the self-serves. So he just asked the lady if she wanted the oil checked, and she said no, and he finished the fill-up and took her credit card. Another full-serve customer, a brown Dodge St. Regis, pulled up just as Marvin got the lady's signature on the credit slip.

It was a busy Monday. So busy that Mr. Sam even had to come out of the service bay to help, glaring at Marvin while he worked on his hands with an oily rag, angry at the interruption of the Spitfire's tune. But Marvin didn't mind. Today was the day *she* came by, driving her little yellow VW Rabbit for its weekly fill-up and oil check.

Marvin unscrewed gas caps and washed windows with a glad heart. The girl's visits always made Mondays special. She was a stunning young woman, a standout even in this land of fabled beach bunnies. Marvin had sketched her many times on his big drawing pad, working patiently from memory. And although he had produced some fine portraits, her next visit invariably revealed some new facet of her beauty that he hadn't quite captured.

Some day, when the drawings were finally right, he would try something in oils. . . .

The service bell dinged.

The yellow Rabbit turned into the station at a little past eight, and Marvin's heart leapt to his throat. She stopped by the diesel pump, which was set on a little concrete island of its own. Marvin trotted over, wiping his hands with one of the heavy-duty paper towels, smiling a happy smile.

He watched her roll down her window, felt his chest tingle when she smiled with recognition. "Oh, hello there."

He grinned and nodded. "Hello to you. Fill 'er up?"

"Please." She handed over the keys to unlock the fuel cap. Marvin went to the pump, unhooked the nozzle, worked the fuel cap with one hand, and slid the nozzle in. He could've set the pump on automatic and gone right to the window-washing bit, but he liked to prolong her visits as much as possible. He squeezed the trigger instead, watching the girl from behind. She was brushing her red hair, her back arched as she peered into the little rearview mirror.

Marvin shook his head in silent admiration. No, his last drawing was all wrong. Her hair was curlier, fuller, and of a far richer lustre than he had conveyed. And her face . . . the last drawing had only made her pretty. She wasn't really pretty at all. The cheekbones were too pronounced, the neck too long and elegant for that simple kind of prettiness. She was more like some exotic Irishwoman of ancient times, a noble's daughter. And her hands. Was there anything in God's green earth more finely made than those hands? He had never really noticed them before, not in all the times she'd been here. But now he would remember. The next drawing would be from the waist up, a three-quarter, with her hands primly folded in her lap. . . .

A little bit of diesel fuel splashed on his shoes and he released the trigger. He knelt and rubbed a paper towel over the fuel that had dribbled along the Rabbit's side. He replaced the nozzle in the pump and took the window washer from its pail. He started with the rear window.

"Oh, that's okay," she called back. Marvin looked at her, surprised. "Don't bother with the windows today. I'm in a real hurry."

He felt his heart sag. "Oh?"

"Here." She extended a twenty. "I'm really late."

He tossed the wiper in its bucket and took the bill. It was crisp, teller-machine fresh. He hurried to the cashbox, made change, and trotted back to the Rabbit and counted it out.

She gave him one last dazzling smile as she rolled up the window. "Thanks again!"

"Sure, so long now."

He watched the Rabbit trundle to the curb. She scooted into the traffic, heading west on Voltaire as always. He knew her destination was UCSD—there were always college textbooks on the passenger seat and there was a student parking sticker on her bumper, current for this semester. He'd had one himself, back before he screwed *that* deal and had to leave, then hosed things all the way by signing up with the goddamn Navy. A stab of anger flicked through his mind, and he worked the rag hard.

"Hey, you! *Boy!*" It was Mr. Sam, bent underneath the opened hood of a Monte Carlo, putting in a quart of oil. "If It ain't too much *trouble*, how about lending a hand, you stupid fu—" He cut off the last word with some difficulty, giving the oil container a little shake to hurry its contents along.

A Mercury Lynx sat on the other side of the full-serve island, its driver impatiently tapping at the wheel. A self-serve customer stood near the cashbox, bills in hand, looking for someone to take his money. Marvin hurried back, the flash of anger gone and forgotten.

He got the nozzle in the Lynx and locked it on automatic, then made change for the self-serve customer. A Thunderbird pulled in line behind the Lynx. A Z-28 Camaro stopped at the self-serves. Marvin took the washer from the pail and cleaned the Lynx's rear window, then went around to hit the front. The nozzle's trigger clicked off, and Marvin squeezed in another thirteen cents' worth to make it an even five. Five! What some people wouldn't do for a free window wash and look under the hood.

Then he took care of the Thunderbird, made change for the guy in the Camaro, and gave directions to a barrel-chested man crammed behind the wheel of a Honda Civic. He checked tire pressures and examined dipsticks, poured water into radiators and batteries, ran MasterCards and Visas through the credit card machine. It was finicky work, and sometimes it was even hard work, but it was not exactly brain work, so Marvin found it easy to devote most of his mind to the brief meeting with the girl.

He tried to reconstruct the scene as it had happened, but all that would come to mind was a series of snapshots, already growing fuzzy and indistinct. Marvin concentrated

21

harder and, as he was checking the tension on a Monte Carlo's fan belt, the images began to do their old trick, melting and shifting until they slowly coalesced into a smooth stream of moving pictures. The girl was behind the wheel of her Rabbit, weaving through the northbound rush-hour traffic on Interstate 5, chin up, sunlight glinting off her Ray-Bans.

"How's it look, kid?" The driver was stuffed into a tight Mexican *guayabera*, complemented by a straw porkpie hat. "Oil okay?"

"Everything's fine, mister." Marvin smiled as he pushed down on the Monte Carlo's hood. "Comes to eighteen-fifty."

Marvin took the money and made change. He watched the Monte Carlo lumber into traffic, feeling that everything was as fine as it could be. The trick had come through again, showing him a picture that was just as sharp and clear as a brand-new Sony Trinitron. He watched the red-headed girl maneuver for the La Jolla Village Drive exit, glancing over her shoulder each time she shifted lanes. . . .

A big Dodge van with a CB antenna pulled into the station. The plates said New Mexico, and the only half-clean part to be seen was where the wipers had cut their swath. He walked toward the van with a smile. He could work and watch the girl at the same time.

It was a talent Marvin rarely thought about. Indeed, he did not look on it as a talent at all; it was something he had just about always been able to do, and he thought it quite as unremarkable as taking a drink from a glass of water. When he'd first learned the word *daydream* he assumed that's what it was. But unlike a daydream, the events he observed unfolded without his slightest control, and when he'd later heard about the strange word *clairvoyance*, he began to wonder if that might be it.

22

But who had there been to ask? His parents? His sister? Teachers? For something like this you needed a friend . . . and besides, he wasn't even sure if the things he saw were really and truly happening.

Sometimes they did. Like the time he had lain awake on a long-ago Christmas Eve and he had closed his eyes and there was his mother before the white aluminum tree, carefully putting together the train tracks. And when he came down the next morning there it was, just as he had seen it, right down to the smoke coming out of the little stack and a real light bulb in the headlight.

But it was also unreliable. Sometimes he tried to make his mind go somewhere or follow someone but nothing would happen. Other times he would see something that turned out not to have happened at all. Like once, back in high school, when some guys had said they would drop by to pick him up to go to a drive-in movie. He had seen them coming down his street clear as a bell, but when he looked out the window the car wasn't there. It never did come, in fact.

Marvin checked the amount of brake fluid in a car's reservoir and took a look at the electrolyte level in a battery. All the while he watched the girl from the perspective of a spy satellite, the kind with a camera sharp enough to read the brand name off a pack of cigarettes. The yellow Rabbit moved through the big parking lot that belonged to Revelle College, finally nosing into a slot at the lot's southern corner. Marvin's perspective changed as the girl got out, dissolving into a closeup that tracked her from behind. He followed her progress across the lot, as she headed into campus between the humanities library and Galathea Hall. She walked quickly, books held tight and high against perfect breasts. Lucky books! He watched her make her way across the broad expanse of Revelle Plaza, where dozens of students in dark glasses were sprawled on the concrete benches, taking in the sun, talking about classes, setting up dates. She went inside the Undergraduate Sciences Building, where he'd spent many an afternoon himself.

She was late, and Marvin frowned as he sensed her distress. It was one of those amphitheater-style classrooms with at least two hundred seats. The students were quiet, bent over their miniature desks, scribbling like mad.

Had to be mid-terms. And the girl was late.

Marvin followed her progress to the auditorium's lecture-stage. There was a bearded young man behind the lectern, some graduate teaching assistant with the job of proctoring. There was writing on the long blackboard, but Marvin couldn't make it come into focus. The girl spoke to the TA, and he smirked as he handed over a mimeographed test. There were lots of empty desks up front. The girl put her books down and opened the test. She bit her lip as she puzzled over the first question.

There was a loud hissing noise. Marvin turned, disoriented, and saw an old Buick Skylark with Mexican plates trundle into the station. Steam was pouring from its hood so thickly that it reminded Marvin of something from a war movie, like a disabled B-25 spiraling down behind enemy lines. He grabbed a wad of oily rags and rushed over, the girl and the classroom completely forgotten.

Marvin popped the hood and steam billowed upward, quickly enveloping him in a warm, moist cloud. Marvin squeezed his eyes tight as he used the rags to grope for the radiator cap. The Mexican driver was somewhere in the background, gibbering in manic Spanish. There was another noise nearby, and Marvin identified it as the cursing of Mr. Sam, shouting urgent instructions. But Marvin knew what to do, and he found the cap and gave it a half-twist. There was a sudden rush of high-pressure steam, and Marvin knew that if he let go of the cap the stuff would shoot straight up and splatter him in a shower of scalding water. But the pent-up pressure spent itself rapidly, and the steam quickly dissipated. Mr. Sam leaned over and peered at the hoses connecting the radiator to the engine.

"There's the pecker," he said mildly. He touched the raditor's return hose, which was wrapped with several turns of aluminum duct tape. "The taco-knocker's in luck. Go get a replacement off the rack and we'll fix this pup right now."

Marvin went off to the service bay, wondering which year he should look up in the GM parts book. Probably '69 or '70. He went to the workbench and opened the thick grease-stained volume and began running his finger down the columns of tiny figures. He thought about the girl again, but the image of the classroom would not materialize. He backtracked and began thinking about the campus itself, hoping to jog things back into motion, but all he could summon up were faded snapshots of the campus, like postcards in a revolving rack at the university bookstore.

Marvin installed the hose, using the original O-clamps. The Mexican carefully counted out the $5.02 that was owed, using three ones and a lot of change. Marvin pointed at the gas pump and then at the Buick's gas cap, eyebrows raised in question. The Mexican checked his battered wallet, then slowly shook his head. Marvin took the water hose and started to fill the radiator, but the Mexican insisted on doing it himself. Marvin turned to a Zephyr sitting by the lead-free. Midway through the fill-up Marvin heard the Mexican crank up—a new muffler was sorely needed—and drive off.

Marvin went on with the business of gassing up and making change, and he doggedly continued to think about the UCSD campus, but the best he could manage was a hazy image of himself a few years before, back when he'd

25

been a student. It had been all right at first, when dear old Dad was picking up the bills. Then not so all right when *that* rug got pulled from under him.

Marvin opened the hood of a Pinto station wagon. The block was black with layers of grease, marred only by the bright orange of a replacement oil filter. He checked the dipstick and the level was a couple of quarts low. Showed the stick to the owner, but got the okay for only one quart. Marvin punched a spout into a can of Pennzoil thirty-weight and twisted off the engine's oil cap.

Yeah, it was too bad he didn't turn out to be smart enough or hardworking enough to swing it all on his own. With two part-time jobs on top of the regular class load, there just didn't seem to be any way. He had tried and he had failed. But that didn't explain why he had been so *stupid*. It didn't explain why he had actually *believed* the crap the Navy recruiter had handed out about the military being so obliging in helping a young man earn his college diploma. . . .

Marvin paused, empty can of Pennzoil in his hand. There she was. He had her again, just as clear as could be, still in the classroom.

He put the oil cap back on and twisted it tight, slammed the hood, and told the driver how much was owed. Marvin grinned as he took the folded bills.

The amphitheater was much busier than before. Time had been called, and students were getting up, putting away pens, filing to the lecture-stage to drop off their tests. But the girl remained at her desk, flipping through the pages she had yet to finish, shaking her head in disbelief. The bearded TA announced time again. The girl's shoulders slumped in resignation. She gathered up her things, closed the test, and made her way through the tide of departing students to the lecture-stage.

Marvin continued with his work, but his mouth was set in an unconscious frown. He watched the girl drop off her test, then melt into the crowd of students heading toward the exit. The amphitheater was off a broad corridor where there was enough room for the crowd to dissipate. But a young man with curly shoulder-length hair remained alongside the girl, one of the surfer boys, smiling and talking and beaming with considerable good cheer. Marvin felt a twinge of anger. The girl wanted to be alone—couldn't the grinning ape see that?

The pair continued down the corridor, the girl paying no attention to the boy. They reached the big double doors at the main entrance, where the multi-arched facade gave onto Revelle Plaza, and the girl stopped, staring straight ahead. The boy continued with his patter, but the girl ignored him, scanning the wide expanse of the plaza as if she were a Cheyenne looking for smoke signals. Then she appeared to make up her mind about something, for she turned around and went back into the building, leaving the boy behind. His face was no longer bright and sunny, but creased with sudden resentment.

The girl did not go far. She went to an unmarked metal door, pushed it open, and passed into a well-lit stairwell. There was a fresh coat of white paint on the concrete walls and the switchbacked staircase was constructed of unadorned steel.

The door slammed behind her, echoing hollowly.

Marvin was so startled he dropped the replacement wiper blade he was preparing to install on a Granada. He bent down and hastily scooped it up, his mind boiling with a mixture of confusion and consternation. Never before had he *heard* anything—not when he was like this, watching someone. Not ever.

He stood and tried to install the blade, but his hands

27

were trembling. He gripped the wiper hard and pushed the blade in, grimacing. He wanted to forget about the girl, at least for a moment. He wanted to be alone to think, to sort out this new development.

But the image would not fade, nor would the sounds. Her high heels made sharp little clicks as she ascended the staircase. She reached the third-story landing and opened the door. There was a long corridor, evenly spaced doors on either side. The girl walked down the carpeted hallway, looking at the plastic nameplates. She stopped at one marked *Prof. Albert Willings.*

Marvin heard the girl knock. There was a muffled reply. She turned the knob and went inside, saying a barely audible hello. A thin, bespectacled man sat behind an untidy desk. His goatee pulled upward as he smiled at the girl. He took the curved pipe from his mouth and motioned to a chair in front of his desk.

Marvin studied the engine compartment of an Isuzu Impulse helplessly. He'd forgotten what he was supposed to be doing. Either checking the oil or the brake fluid level, one of the two. Or was it the window washing reservoir? Whatever, the compartment seemed vague and unreal in comparison with the laser-sharp rendering of the professor's office. He could even read the scrawl across one of the squares of the Garfield calendar: *Dr. Wheeler 2:30 SHARP!!* A large fern hung near the half-opened window, its fronds shifting lazily in the breeze. The girl talked quietly, and though the words were unclear, Marvin could pick up the tone. She was upset about something, almost desperate.

The professor, on the other hand . . . Marvin decided there wasn't something quite right about him. Here was a troubled girl, and he was acting as if he were listening to an amusing story, smiling and nodding, seemingly more concerned with the slow ritual of refilling his pipe. Perfectly nonchalant . . . except for the look in his eyes. There was something there more than polite interest. Something that reminded Marvin of the boy who'd talked with the girl earlier.

He closed the Isuzu's hood, banging it down hard. He told the driver everything was fine and took a five and two ones for the gas. He walked to the cashbox, jammed the small key into the lock, and cursed when it did not open right away.

Marvin continued to watch the scene in the professor's office, a vague feeling of anger and unease percolating in his mind. The professor got out of his chair, and Marvin could see that a little roll of fat pressed over his belt buckle. The professor went to the window and stared at the view, taking the pipe from his mouth to say something in a fatherly tone. He glanced over his shoulder at the girl, and she mumbled a reply as she wiped her nose with a Kleenex. His eyes flickered to where her skirt was hiked midway up her thigh. She put the tissue down and looked up at him, saying something and shaking her head. The professor smiled and walked toward the front of his desk—giving her shoulder a reassuring pat as he passed by—and parked his haunch on a corner of the desk. The girl continued talking as she searched through her purse for another tissue. The professor sucked on his pipe and nodded. His eyes flickered to her legs.

Marvin's anger was no longer smoldering. It was more like a piece of coal, glowing brighter, getting ready to ignite. And mixed in with the anger was nausea, rolling over him in a greasy wave. He became conscious of the breakfast he'd hastily eaten, and how uneasily it now sat in his stomach. His face felt sweaty. He looked at the side of the gas station, where the bathrooms were, and thought it might be a good idea to take a walk over there, just to splash some cold water on his face.

Marvin passed a hand over his forehead, but the sweaty feeling did not go away. A van slid up to the full-serve and the bell dinged, but Marvin ignored it. He began walking toward the bathrooms. He fumbled his key into the lock and went inside the tiny room, closed the lid on the toilet, and sat down. He put his face in his hands and moaned. The overpowering aroma of the urinal's deodorant cake sent his stomach into a looping barrel roll.

He tried to stop watching the scene in the professor's office, but . . . the girl was crying now, her shoulders bobbing up and down. The professor put his pipe down and leaned over, placing his hand on her arm, saying something soothing.

The piece of coal glowed, surrounded now by a halo of flame. Marvin's stomach clenched unpleasantly.

The professor slipped off the desk and knelt beside the girl. He patted her shoulders. He began . . . kissing her, pressing his lips against her cheek and then drawing away, muttering something softly, then kissing her again. . . . The charcoal burned bright and hot now. The professor moved closer, maneuvering his face so that he could kiss her full on the lips. . . . He placed his hands on either side of her lovely head and began pressing hard, working his way in. The girl shook her head and tried to push away, and he came off his knees as he grabbed at her . . . and Marvin gasped when a new sound burst into his head, a machine-gun angry sound that at first made no sense then all of a sudden came through, loud and clear, as hammering words—

Christ, what's needed is for someone to bust down that goddamn door and really lay into that professor, pick

him up by the collar of his tweedy jacket, slam him up against the wall and start slapping the living shit out of him, change that surprised look on his face to terror, get down heavy-duty with teaching old teach a lesson, and even if the girl gets in the way and tries to stop it, just shove her out of the way and get on with, no reason to stop because a girl doesn't have the stomach for what is needed, and man, what scum like this needs is never very pretty, no, never very pretty at all—

Marvin got off the toilet quickly. He flipped the lid up and leaned over and the professor's office finally left his mind as the half-digested food came barreling up out of his stomach and spewed out into the water below and there was a hammering at the bathroom's door and Mr. Sam was yelling what the fuck's going on in there you goddamn fuckpoke you think I'm paying you four dollars an hour to sit around blowing your goddamn groceries?

□

T H R E E

Marvin straightened up, telling Mr. Sam he'd be just a minute. He steadied himself against the wash basin and turned on the cold water. There was a low-pressure dribble into the porcelain basin, and Marvin splashed water on his face, sighing. Then he splashed his face again.

There was a fresh round of banging at the door, making the frame tremble. Marvin turned the water off and opened the door. Mr. Sam stood just outside, glaring hard enough to crack boulders. Marvin wiped his mouth with the back of his hand, wishing he'd had the chance to rinse out his mouth.

"You get your business done, boy?"

Marvin nodded slowly. He glanced down at his shirt, checking to see if there was any vomit, and wiped off a speck.

"Some idiot's asking directions to someplace I never heard of, and that kind of thing's your department." Mr. Sam smiled grimly, lowering his voice. "That is, of course, if'n you don't *mind* taking a little time out to do your fucking job."

Marvin walked back to the service islands, his stomach rumbling uneasily. The image of the girl was utterly gone, and Marvin didn't care. All he wanted was a place to sit down and a cold Coke to sip. He told the driver of a show-room-new Fiat X1-9 how to get to the freeway and which exit to take for Mt. Palomar. He gassed up an old Volkswagen bus whose sides bore the faint tracings of a sunset mural, painted long ago. He made change for a plump young man who wore a Teledyne Ryan ID badge clipped to his breast pocket. He filled up an Oldsmobile diesel, and when the engine turned over the heavy fumes brought the nausea back in waves. He leaned against the island's stanchion, looking down at the window-washing bucket, wondering if he might loose it again.

"Marvy *boy!*" There was a hard slap against Marvin's back, making him stagger off the island. "What'sa matter, Marv? Little too much *partying* last night?"

The voice belonged to Dell Ready, who, along with J.J. Mirando, rounded out Mr. Sam's work force. They were just reporting for duty.

"Big ol' beach stud like you's probably screwing his brains out all the live-long night." Dell had a deep, rumbling chuckle. "Ain't that right?"

33

Marvin kept his eyes averted, wishing the twitching in his cheek would go away. Dell's chuckling suddenly tapered off.

"I said, ain't that right, Marv?"

Marvin looked up. Dell was unsmiling now, his thumbs hooked through the loops of his oil-crudded jeans. He was a biker, age indeterminate, with small gray eyes. J.J. was standing just behind Dell, wearing a half-hearted grin, and quickly looked away before Marvin caught his eye.

"Yeah, Dell, that's right."

All signs of mirth had left the biker's eyes. "What a fucking dip," he said evenly. "C'mon, J.J. Let's hit it."

The pair headed toward the service bays, Dell's ponytail bouncing between his shoulder blades.

A little red Omni Miser by the full-serve island beeped its horn, and Marvin hurried over.

Mr. Sam's idea of good looks in a man would have satisfied a Marine drill instructor, but Dell Ready could have been covered with green stars and polka dots for all he cared. Dell was that rarity of rarities—a pure, natural-born mechanic, the kind that quickly builds a customer-drawing reputation. His price was right, too; a fifty-fifty split on the labor charge, with five percent commission on parts.

Dell had had roughly the same arrangement at other gas stations without number, and it was a livelihood that suited him perfectly. There was usually enough wampum in his money belt at any given time to pull stakes and hit the bricks, heading his mint-condition '63 Harley Duo Glide out on the aimless journey he had begun when he was fourteen. And whenever the cash ran low there wasn't a town in America where he couldn't find work.

He'd been in San Diego more than a year now, a record, and was coming up on his sixth month with Mr. Sam. San

Diego had started off pretty good, but he was finding there was only so much sunshine and palm trees a man could take. And the sweet little mama he'd linked up with had turned into a fat cow mama now that she was pregnant— and it probably wasn't his kid to boot. To put the icing on the cake, he'd invested heavily in a sure-fire cocaine deal that'd gone as sour as sour could get, costing him his entire $5,500 nest egg when the Coast Guard fired shots across the bow of that "uncatchable" speedboat.

J.J. Mirando, a compactly built Chicano, was Dell's work-mate and understudy. At age thirty-three he was making a superhuman effort to unfuck his life. He had strong mo-tivation to succeed, for if he screwed up the job with Mr. Sam he knew he'd start screwing up everything else, and his probation officer had made it very clear he wouldn't hesitate to have J.J. finish out the four-to-six he'd been serv-ing at Chino. But bad as that was, what was worse was what might become of his daughter. She'd been born with a club foot, and MediCal did not cover all the therapy that was required. J.J. was only a mediocre mechanic, but his desperation to succeed made up for much. He worked for a straight wage—five dollars an hour—but had high hopes for taking over Dell's slot when he left.

In the course of a day, J.J. assisted Dell on the big jobs until Dell wrapped up at six or seven, then handled the pumps until closing time at eleven. Marvin Moy usually knocked off at three, unless there was overtime, and Mr. Sam took a two- or three-hour break in the late afternoon to refresh himself for the night shift. That was the usual routine. But today would be different.

The police came at two-thirty.

It was a white Ford LTD, standard-issue for the San Diego Police Department. It pulled into one of the parking slots next to the station office, and two officers got out. One wore a tailored khaki uniform, the other was plainclothes.

Marvin finished gassing up a gray Pulsar, studying the cops from the corner of his eye. This was the second time he'd seen policemen at the service station; the first had been over a year ago, something about a missing person, and they'd been in and out in less than a minute. This looked different, somehow, like the cops were intent on some business close at hand. *Real* close at hand. Marvin made change for the Pulsar's pretty driver and gave a barely audible thanks. He took a paper towel from the island's dispenser and, though his hands weren't dirty, began working the towel uneasily.

Mr. Sam met them by the Coke machine. They all shook hands. Then they talked. Finally, Mr. Sam gave a decisive nod and pointed Marvin's way.

Marvin froze in astonishment. His bowels felt loose and watery. The cops began walking toward him, Mr. Sam trailing grimly behind. The plainclothesman reached him first. His brown hair was carefully styled, covering his forehead and the tops of his ears. Big, thick mustache and oval aviator sunglasses. He was chewing gum, his mouth slightly open. "You Marvin Moy?"

"Yes, sir."

The cop looked Marvin up and down. He took his time about it, like a rancher examining a new piece of horseflesh. Marvin continued to work on his hands with the paper towel. The uniformed cop, taller than Marvin and of more considerable heft, watched the scene impassively. The silence seemed overly long.

"My name's Sergeant Perry," he said at last. He didn't bother to introduce the patrolman. "I'm a detective with the San Diego Police Department."

"Yes, sir?"

"Your boss here, Mr. Hattstaedt, he says you've been working here all day."

Marvin swallowed drily. "Yes, sir. I came on duty at quarter to seven."

"Been here ever since," Mr. Sam added from the background. He seemed kind of sour and pissed off, as if this little episode was draining off valuable time, but his watery blue eyes were bright and intent.

The sergeant nodded. He had his hands on his hips, checked jacket spread to reveal a wide but not soft-looking gut. "Know a young lady by the name of Genevieve Collier?"

"N-no . . ." Marvin's brow creased in concentration. "No, sir."

"Real nice-looking gal. Redhead."

Marvin stopped working the paper towel.

"Drives a little yellow Rabbit," Perry continued. "A diesel."

"I think so." Marvin licked his lips. "I mean, there *is* a girl like that, with red hair. Brings her Rabbit here every Monday. But I don't know her. I never even knew her name until you just mentioned it."

Sergeant Perry worked his gum more vigorously. " 'Kay. Now, you ever hear of a professor out at UCSD, a guy by the name of Al Willings?"

Marvin was about to say no when a '65 Mustang with a shot muffler rumbled into the station, making a din that drowned out the ding of the service bell. Mr. Sam yelled out for J.J. to get his ass on over to the Mustang and take the hell care of it. The engine finally coughed out, making the regular street noise seem hushed, or, Marvin thought, like what some people called *oppressive*; he felt a queasy disorientation, and wondered what this man was doing here with his huge aviator sunglasses, staring at him and chewing gum and finally moving his lips to form the words, "Well, Marv, do you or don't you?"

"Do I . . . do I what?"

"*Know* Willings?"

Marvin looked away. "No. No, sir, Sergeant. I never heard of him."

Perry slowed his gum-chewing way down. Sunlight glinted dully off his dark glasses. "You don't lie too good, asshole."

"I'm not ly-lying!" Marvin brought the level of his voice down. "I mean, you know, I used to be a student at UCSD . . . and I . . . I don't know, maybe I might've had him for one of my classes. Maybe I . . ."

He let the words trail off. The nausea had come back, and he wondered what he must look like to Sergeant Perry, with his eyes as wide as silver dollars and sweat beading out on his forehead.

Like the guiltiest son of a bitch in the world, that's how.

"So what if he knows this professor?" Mr. Sam broke in, peeved. "What is it you're trying to get at?"

Perry did not take his eyes off Marvin. He began chewing his gum rapidly again, and it seemed as if his gut was closing in on Marvin's space. "Seems there was an assault." The sergeant's voice was as hard and flat as a rock. "Seems someone busted down Professor Willings' office door, and then proceeded to beat the pure living dogshit out of him. He's in the hospital now." Sergeant Perry stepped even closer, and Marvin backed off. "Slammed him up against the wall. Broke his goddamn *jaw*. Miss Collier witnessed the whole thing. And she described you to a tee, *Mr*. Moy."

Marvin took another step back, but the pavement seemed to roll like the deck of a small sailboat. He put his hand to his brow to wipe away the sweat, and the pavement started to yaw and slip, now more like the inside of the Fun Tunnel

38

at the Del Mar Fair, and the sun swung down to the center of his vision, blotting out everything with an overwhelming brilliance.

Marvin came to in the service station office, slumped in the rickety swivel chair. Mr. Sam was squeezing a damp paper towel so that cold water dribbled over Marvin's forehead. He sat up, shaking his head.

"Here you go, sonny." Sergeant Perry extended a frosty can of orange Nehi. Marvin accepted the can and took a tentative sip. Found that Perry had already drunk half of it.

"You feel okay now?" Perry was sitting on a corner of Mr. Sam's desk, legs dangling. The tall uniformed cop was in the background, leaning against the doorjamb.

"Yeah, I think so . . ." Marvin ran a hand through his thinning hair. "Feel a lot better, thank you, Sergeant."

Perry pasted on a solicitous grin. "Listen, sorry if I was a little too hard-nosed out there."

Marvin shrugged diffidently.

"I mean, I guess I've kind of forgotten what it's like to be your age. College can be a real pressure-cooker, and, well, it just kind of aggravates things when a professor has it in for you. Right?"

Marvin looked up. "None of the professors had it in for me."

"You know, it wouldn't be any problem to check your records. Find out how many classes you had from Willings. What sort of grades he gave you."

Marvin spread his hands. "Check them all you want. Honest, I'm not even sure if I ever *had* him."

"Believe me, you'll feel a whole world better when you get it off your chest."

"There's nothing to get off! I mean, I'm fine, really. Nothing's bothering me."

Perry grinned harder. "Sure. That's why you handled things so well out there."

Mr. Sam broke in. "He *has* been feeling poorly, Sergeant. I caught him blowing chow just a couple hours ago."

Doubt crossed Perry's face. He chewed his gum slowly and thoughtfully.

"Look, Sergeant." Marvin had a hopeful look on his face. "Maybe you could take me to see Miss Collier, in person. I'm sure that'd clear it up."

Perry's forehead wrinkled. He had, in fact, been planning to ask the boy to do just that. Even though his alibi was airtight, his reaction to the news of the assault was interesting enough to overlook the alibi . . . at least temporarily. Or long enough to let the girl meet this Moy character and see what might happen. He cleared his throat. "Why do you want to see her?"

"I just . . ." Marvin's cheeks flushed, and he looked down. "I want to see if she's, you know, okay."

So Moy had a crush on the girl, Perry thought. Well, how about that? Another little something to add to the hopper. He looked at Mr. Sam. "We're taking Marv for a drive, pops."

"That so?" Mr. Sam looked as if he was getting ready to argue the point, but he turned his scowl on Marvin. "You know I have to dock you for this, don't you?"

"Uh, sure thing, Mr. Sam."

Thank Christ I don't work here, Perry thought. The old coot looks like a regular ball buster. "We won't be long. We're just heading over to Scripps."

"Scripps?" Marvin asked. He was getting up slowly from the chair. "Scripps Hospital?"

"Yeah. She has a concussion. Seems Miss Collier kind of got in the way during the fracas." He watched Marvin intently. "Got a little banged around while the professor was

40

getting his . . . well, you know how these things can get out of hand."

The color drained from Marvin's face. He wavered like a tree getting ready to fall, and Perry thought he actually would.

But he didn't. Marvin followed them out to the cruiser, walking a little stiff-legged.

Marvin sat in back, separated from the officers by a heavy-duty wire-mesh screen. They drove in silence, save for the occasional squawk from the dispatcher, each alone with their thoughts.

The uniformed officer, an ambitious patrolman by the name of Buddy Gray, was trying not to think about his next-door neighbor's lucious young wife. But her green eyes had the damndest way of sneaking into his thoughts when he could least afford it. Like now, when he should have been mulling over Sergeant Perry's interrogation techniques, which he needed to know for the Detective Examination Board. *If* he went before the board, that was. And how good was Perry, anyway? They said he was pretty good on Homicide—the big time—but there was the awesome fact that he couldn't hack it over the long haul and had been transferred to Assaults and Robberies.

Buddy sighed. The luscious one's husband was supposedly out of town tonight, and his own wife was safely gone, visiting her folks up in Seattle. Next-door-neighbor lady had been giving him all kinds of looks over the backyard fence lately, little pink tongue kind of flicking out and rolling over her lips. . . . Buddy Gray's hands began to get sweaty on the wheel.

Anton Perry stared straight ahead, unseeing, thinking about how Moy had passed out. And the way he had lied when he said he didn't know that professor guy. And about

41

all the other times in his eight years as a detective that one of those ironclad alibis had turned out to be nothing more than baling wire and Silly Putty. Mr. Sam said that Moy had gone off to the bathroom to barf sometime during the morning. It was eight miles from the gas station to UCSD. Let's say the kid got on something that was really souped-up and made every light. There was a likely item sitting in back of the station, that old Harley Duo Glide. Let's say Moy borrowed it for a little while. Ten, twelve minutes each way? With maybe five minutes to pound the shit out of the good professor?

Perry sighed, sinking lower into the seat. Not fucking likely. Someone would've seen Moy leaving; certainly that biker punk who owned the hog. So scratch that. But Moy *had* to be involved, somehow. The girl's description had been very precise, even though she'd been a little looney when she'd given it. And you didn't have to be a grade-A squared-away hotshit detective to see that Moy was guilty about *something*.

Perry worried at the problem, trying different angles. It was procedure he was well accustomed to, mostly due to long evenings of chess with his wife, rather than the cases he'd worked. The jams she'd get him into! The endgames! He'd given her one of those little computerized chess games two Christmases ago, and she was dicking around with the grandmaster setting the very same day. When she deigned to play with him he rarely had a good time, but he'd learned to look beyond the despair of the moment and keep butting his head against the puzzle. And, as often as not, he found a way to untangle himself.

Marvin sat hunched forward, staring at his thumbnails. Thoughts tumbled through his mind like the spinning wheels in a slot machine, only instead of the blurred images of bars, bells, and fruit, there were the whirring registers of police, the assault they'd reported, and the girl who now had a lovely name to go with a lovely face. . . .

Marvin sat back in the seat and detected the faint aroma of some kind of industrial-strength cleaner. Now that they were on the interstate, the land to either side was rolling hills of scrub, largely undeveloped. He spotted the top floors of Scripps Memorial over the rise of a grassy hill, and the cruiser eased into the exit lane.

Marvin bit his thumbnail. *Had* things gone on in the professor's office just as he'd . . . seen? And why had he become ill just as the assault was supposed to have taken place? Marvin sighed. He'd become ill because of the professor's advances on Genevieve, of course. It was enough to make anyone sick. A professor making advances on a student! Perhaps the police should be investigating *that*. Perhaps the attacker should be looked on more as a *saviour* instead of a—

Marvin held onto the idea. A saviour . . . that was more like it. That Genevieve had been injured was just an unfortunate accident. *She* had known she was being rescued. And when the police had asked for a description of her saviour, in her confusion she had naturally . . . come up with the man at the gas station . . . with whom she was secretly in love.

The patrol car pulled into a slot marked "For Medical Staff Only." Marvin felt his pulse quicken. He was actually going to meet her. And she would finally learn his name.

They got out, and Marvin did not notice how quickly Patrolman Gray took up position just to his right. All three were in step as they walked down the wide portico of the main entranceway. The lobby was small, hung with oil paintings, and there was real furniture instead of plastic chairs. Sergeant Perry smiled at the gray-haired receptionist. "Me again."

She smiled at him with recognition but looked at the newcomers with wary interest. "Good afternoon, Detective Perry."

"Is Dr. Franklin available?"

"I don't know, but I can certainly have him paged."

"I'd appreciate it." Perry stepped toward the elevator bank and pressed the up button. Two of the three doors immediately rumbled open. "When you get in touch please tell him that we're on our way up to Miss Collier's room."

"Why, ah . . . of course." She watched the three uncertainly.

Sergeant Perry hit the fifth floor button as the door accordioned closed. "Can't tell you how much I appreciate your coming with us, Marvin. Makes things a lot easier."

"Yes, sir." He took off his grease-stained Padres cap. "No problem, really."

Perry watched how Marvin handled the cap. Like some turn-of-the-century suitor fidgeting with a straw hat, he told himself. He smiled, turning his attention to the creeping light of the floor indicator. It hit five, and there was a momentary surge of semi-weightlessness. Then the doors slid open.

Marvin felt his heart beat even faster as they stepped out of the elevator. The great moment was almost at hand. They went to the nurses' station, where they were met by a doctor whose white jacket set off his tanned, merry face. Marvin watched as the sergeant and the doctor conferred in hushed tones. Then he found himself walking down another long corridor, the doctor leading the way. Marvin ran his hand through his hair, wishing there was some way he could ask to go to the bathroom to tidy up.

The doctor opened the door to a small three-bed ward.

44

The room was bright with the full light of mid-afternoon, making the drapes of the privacy curtains glow luminously.

Only the far bed was occupied. The top of Genevieve's head was tightly wrapped in bandages, her lovely red hair splayed wide over the pillow. She was looking out the window, lying perfectly still, and as they approached, Marvin saw that not even her eyelids moved.

The air went out of his lungs, leaving a sweetly tingling vacuum. *Dear God, is there anything in this world more beautiful than this woman?*

The doctor spoke to Genevieve, but Marvin couldn't hear what was said. He gripped his cap tightly and leaned forward expectantly. Genevieve began turning her head. Slowly. So slowly. There was a bruise under her right eye. She looked at the sergeant without recognition, then took in the patrolman. Then her green eyes came to rest on Marvin.

Marvin smiled shyly, nodding.

Her eyes widened a little as she smiled. She started to push herself up, but Dr. Franklin put a gentle hand on her shoulder.

"Please, dear. You must remain very still."

She flashed an angry look at the doctor and knocked his hand away. Marvin tensed. Then things started happening very quickly.

Genevieve tried to scrabble out of bed, awkwardly at first as she fought with the sheets, but picking up momentum. The doctor grabbed both of her shoulders and tried to push her down, but she swung her knee into his groin. The doctor stumbled back against the wall. Sergeant Perry grabbed her arm just as she tumbled off the bed, and they both went down together. Marvin rushed around the corner of the bed, desperately anxious.

The doctor and the policeman had her by each arm now, hauling her up. Marvin suddenly found himself face-to-face

45

with the girl, but she wasn't pretty anymore. She looked at Marvin with terror and loathing, and her mouth was wide with a noise that quickly built into a shriek, the sound becoming so godawful loud that Marvin had to back off, hands clapped to his ears.

□

F O U R

They returned to the gas station twenty minutes later. Marvin was halfway out of the cruiser when Sergeant Perry turned around and spoke through the wire mesh. "Thanks again, Marv. Sorry it turned out the way it did."

Marvin nodded absently, one hand on the door.

"You see, I thought she was a lot better off than she was. Even the doc thought she was doing pretty good." Sergeant Perry looked pained. "Had I known she was as crazy as a bugboard, I wouldn't have counted her description of you

47

or anyone else for jack. I sure wouldn't have taken you to see her."

Marvin looked down at the oily concrete.

"Listen, I wouldn't get racked up over this. It's unfortunate she . . . well, *confused* you with whoever really made the assault. If I were you I'd try to forget all about it."

Marvin's jaws were clenched tight. He nodded stiffly.

Some distance away Mr. Sam was in the process of checking under the hood of a blue Capri. It was a chore that only had half his attention; mostly he was concerned with the trio in the police cruiser. He saw Marvin get out and shut the door. Mr. Sam recapped the battery and slammed the hood. He went around to the driver's window and told him everything was fine and collected eight singles for the gas. He saw Marvin walking toward the rear of the gas station, where the battered little B-210 was parked.

Mr. Sam pocketed the money as he walked after Marvin. He couldn't believe the son of a bitch was going back to his cruddy Datsun, just like that, without so much as a how-do-you-do. "Hey, Marv!" He felt himself getting angrier by the second. *"Marv!"*

The young man stopped and turned around. The look on his face froze Mr. Sam at ten yards. It was a look he hadn't seen in years—not since Korea, when positions were being overrun and ammo was low.

Mr. Sam was so shocked and confused that he stared. He didn't know for how long, but Marvin eventually turned his back and walked on to the rear of the station. Presently there was the whinny of the Datsun's aging starter, and the engine finally caught.

Mr. Sam patted at his mouth with an oily rag. He tried to remember what he'd been so all-fired eager to talk about with Marvin. After all, it *was* a good half-hour past the boy's quitting time. Had every right to get home as quick as he could. Mr. Sam wiped the sweat from his brow. There'd be plenty of time to talk with the boy tomorrow. . . .

The trip home was interminable, each stoplight and clogged intersection feeding his rage. He leaned on the horn, floored the accelerator, and banged on the dash when some fucking asshole tourist drove too goddamn slow. He squealed into the alleyway behind the Cota Arms, making an old spotted dog yelp as it skittered out of the way, and was out of the car before the engine finished coughing out.

He walked toward the back gate swiftly, telling himself they'd be selling Icee Cones in the center of Hell before he thought about that red-haired bitch again. He passed through the gate and saw that someone had placed one of the trash cans halfway in front of his staircase, not taking the trouble to put it another yard over where it was supposed to be. He gave it a sidelong kick as he passed by, and the can thumped over and rolled into the alley, leaving a sodden trail of empty milk cartons, egg shells, and coffee grounds. He took the stairs three at a time, each heavy thud making the old wooden structure tremble.

He kicked his front door and it banged open. He walked into his apartment with his head lowered, his eyes tiny slits. No, Marvin told himself, he wasn't going to think about that bitch anymore because he had something important to do. Something *urgent*. He went over to his drawing table —a big piece of plywood he'd found in the alley, propped up on two sawhorses—and began rummaging though the pile of drawings. Seascapes and birds and carefully drawn copies of *Rolling Stone* cover photographs floated to the floor, and Marvin grew impatient as he dug through the pile, scattering big pieces of newsprint in a widening circle.

Then he found what he was looking for and held it up, grinning. It was the most recent sketch of dear little Miss

49

Collier, a little head-and-shoulders number. How sweet! How pure! How *innocent!* Not at all like the haggard banshee who'd pointed at him and screamed loud enough to bring the duty nurses all the way from the other end of the hallway! No, sir! This here was nothing more than a *cunt* who really deserved nothing so much as a—a—

He tore it down the middle with one savage yank, then brought the two pieces together to tear them into fourths, then eighths, then sixteenths, then the picture disintegrated into two wads of paper in each clenched fist, and Marvin tore at each batch with such manic fury that little pieces began to fly off in a fine spray of confetti, and he tore and tore until there was nothing left in his hands.

Then he was still. He stared at the torn pieces on the floor, eyes blank, unthinking. Feeling like . . . like . . .

. . . he'd just woken up from one of those dreams. . . .

He sank to the littered floor slowly, like an old man, and put his face in his hands.

It was late afternoon by the time Marvin finished tidying up. The last thing set to rights was the oil painting he'd been dabbling with off and on for the past several weeks. He picked up the rickety little aluminum easel and reset the legs, then picked up the canvas board.

He shook his head as he examined it. The painting was crude, almost malformed. Oils were a lot different than pencil and charcoal—they were difficult. Maybe even impossibly difficult. He might never get the hang of it.

He changed into shorts and a sweatshirt. He decided he would head down to Sunrise Grocer's and pick up some natural-type food, eat it at the beach, then come back and see if his little black-and-white was in the mood for catching any channels tonight. Maybe even pick up a six-pack.

He left the apartment, and as he closed the door he heard the sound of a trash can being uprighted, accompanied by muted cursing. He went downstairs quickly, suddenly reminded of his trash-can-kicking incident. If only he'd remembered sooner. . . .

There was a woman in the alley squatting on her haunches, picking up stray bits of trash. It was Miss Ontiveros, the Cota Arms' manager. She heard Marvin's footsteps and turned her face upward, her eyes an angry green.

"You do this?" A soggy coffee filter dangled between her thumb and forefinger. "You the one who tossed all this shit around?"

Marvin stopped midway down the staircase. He could feel his face redden.

Miss Ontiveros stood and flicked the used coffee filter in the trash. She wiped her hands. "Thanks a hell of a lot, wise-ass." Strands of brown hair hung across her face, and she was not the type of woman who became prettier with anger. "This really does great things for the neighborhood, you know? Shows everyone how much class we've got."

Marvin continued walking down. "I'm sorry, really. I was just . . . in such a hurry . . ."

"Yeah. Sure." Miss Ontiveros tossed her head so that strands flicked out of the way. "Bet you also forget to wipe your ass when you're in a hurry."

Marvin avoided her eyes as he hunkered down and began picking up the remaining trash. He could feel her eyes on his back, and he was horribly embarrassed. Up until now he'd been a good tenant. All the manager had known about him was that he was the quiet guy who paid the rent on time. Now he would be known as the *pig* who lived out back.

He picked up a broken wine bottle and tossed it in the

can, collected soggy pieces of paper towel and a dripping yogurt carton. Then, out of the corner of his eye, he saw that Miss Ontiveros was kneeling too, picking up little bits of broken glass and flicking them into the can.

They worked in silence. It was the longest Marvin had ever been in Miss Ontiveros's presence, despite the fact she'd been collecting his rent every month for the past two years. She always gave him a nice smile when he delivered the check, but those glimpses had been fleeting, the smiles formal. All he knew about her was that she had a lovely figure and liked to keep to herself.

When the trash was finally collected, they each took a handle of the can and carried it to its customary spot near the back gate.

"There. All done." She wiped her hands against her jeans and glanced at Marvin. He quickly looked away.

"I'm really sorry about all this," he said quietly.

"Oh, it really wasn't that bad." Her tone was surprisingly friendly—or at least it wasn't hostile. Marvin raised his eyes to meet hers. She was looking at him speculatively, arms folded under her breasts. She honestly did have a nice figure, Marvin thought. Really a knockout. But he noticed with some surprise that tiny wrinkles fanned from the corners of her eyes, and the brown hair contained strands of gray.

"Now I know what I was trying to remember about you." She smiled hesitantly. "You're the one who slipped the note under my door, weren't you? About the plumbing?"

"Yeah, that was me." He looked down at the pavement. " 'Bout a month ago, I guess. The water pressure seems like it's getting less and less. Now all I get out of the shower is just a dribble."

"If it was getting worse why didn't you come to see me?"

He shrugged.

"Well, I've learned enough from this job to be a halfway

52

decent plumber. Let's go take a look at it; maybe I can fix it myself."

"Only if it's no trouble, Miss Ontiveros."

She smiled broadly. "Kathryn. And it's no trouble. I'm the manager, after all."

"Okay . . . Kathryn."

Marvin opened the door and stood aside. Kathryn noticed the sharp odor of turpentine first, then the painting on the aluminium easel, then the piles of drawings on the big work table.

"Oh, my. I didn't know you were an artist."

He looked embarrassed. "Oh, no, not at all. I just, you know, fool around with it. . . ."

She couldn't take her eyes off the portrait on the easel. It was a fantastic piece of work, executed with all the subtlety of a jackhammer. The lines were bold, the colors applied directly from the tube, the face huge and brooding. "I should say you more than fool around with it. Self-portrait?"

He shrugged, smiling. "Can't afford a model."

Kathryn moved to the long work table. The drawings there were in stark contrast to the painting—studied, draftsman-like, well-executed—but not nearly so interesting as the painting.

"What's this?" Kathryn picked up a piece of the torn drawing.

Marvin took it from her hand and tossed it into the wastebasket. "Nothing. Something that didn't work out."

"Oh. Well, let's have a look at the plumbing."

Kathryn watched Marvin demonstrate the low pressure in the shower and in the sink, but her mind wasn't on it. She was thinking about the painting. It was really as good as anything she'd seen in a commercial gallery. Perhaps better. And what was it that Marvin Moy did for a living? Pump gas at a service station, or something like that?

"Well, what do you think?"

"Hm? Oh. It might just be something with the main valve outside. Let's go check."

Marvin followed Kathryn downstairs. There was a faucet against the base of the garage, with a garden hose attached to it. The faucet was set on a pipeline that came up from the ground and ran into the garage on an elbow joint. Directly underneath the faucet was a valve, and Kathryn started turning its knob. "Hey, shit, whaddya know. Here's the problem."

"Huh?"

She finished turning it open. "This is the cutout valve for your water supply. Some jerk must've gotten confused when they used the hose. Ended up turning the wrong knob."

Marvin stared at the connection. The knobs for the faucet and the cutout were exactly the same. And his low-pressure problems hadn't started until just after he'd washed his Datsun. . . .

"Thanks a million," he said. "I should've checked on this before I bothered you."

She stood, wiping her hands, smiling warmly. "No problem at all. Really."

Their business was done, but Marvin didn't want it to end. He wondered what she would say if he . . . invited her to go with him to the beach. For a walk. Sure, and then maybe hit one of the beachfront delicatessens for a couple of sandwiches. Maybe wash them down with some Mexican beer.

Marvin grinned hesitantly. "Well, be seeing you. Sorry about the trouble, Kathryn."

She smiled. "Sure. See you."

Marvin trudged through the powdery sand, heading directly for the surf line. The sun was down and dusk was gathering, but there was still enough light for some die-hard volleyballers near the lifeguard station. Several concrete fire pits dotted the upper part of the beach, and cookouts were underway.

He shifted the small paper bag to his other hand. Inside was din-din, two macrobiotic raisin-nut cupcakes and a small plastic bottle of carrot juice. He glanced at the lithe figures of the volleyball players as he walked by. He pretended for a moment that he was one of them, waiting in happy anticipation for the tall blonde's serve, warm in the knowledge that soon there would be beer-drinking and wienie-roasting by one of the fires.

If only he had enough guts to walk up and say hello. But so what? Even if he did—he knew from time-tested experience—their friendly smiles would change to the cool expressions of the chosen special and their ranks would grow tight as they froze out the interloper.

Marvin trudged on and was soon on the better footing of the densely packed sand of the lower beach. He turned right, heading north. A wave rolled and crashed, and there was a sizzling hiss as the rushing foam played itself out. There was a good breeze, and he could feel strands of hair playing about his head.

Friends. He had never really made any in high school, unless you counted the usual clustering together of gawky misfits. But he never even fit in with that group, forever set apart by a lack of interest in Dungeons & Dragons and science fiction novels . . . and by his imposing physical presence, so unlike theirs.

Coach Ramsey liked the looks of him, though. Or "the cut of his jib," as he was fond of booming out. He hustled

Marvin into a football tryout during his junior year, and it proved a total disaster before it got an inch off the ground. Marvin had been standing in line with a bunch of other guys in their sweats, slowly moving along as each guy at the head of the line took off and tried their hand at catching the long bomb. He'd just been standing there, watching a guy run out under a pass, when Wyatt Edwards came up from behind. He'd just caught his ball and was running to the next station when he stopped and yelled *Hey, Marv!* And Marvin had turned around—wasn't, in fact, even fully turned around—when the ball came rocketing into his gut. Marvin was totally unprepared, and his stance was awkward enough so that he doubled up and fell backward, and there was laughter, plenty of it, and even Coach Ramsey had a few good-natured chuckles as everyone pointed at the big dumb kid who couldn't even take a little four-foot toss without falling flat on his ass. . . .

Marvin reached the basalt jetty and climbed up. It was full evening now, but the stars were few and dull, especially in comparison to the tiny warning strobes of a high-flying passenger plane. He reached the top of the jetty and surveyed the upper part of the beach; three widely spaced cookouts were going full bore, and he could see miniature silhouettes of long-haired girls and lanky young men roasting hot dogs, drinking beers, horsing around. Marvin climbed down and continued his northward trek.

High school graduation had come shortly before his eighteenth birthday. That same fall he was a freshman at the University of California, San Diego. Dad took care of the tuition, along with the curriculum. He had, in fact, sat in on Marvin's first interview with his academic advisor, making sure there wouldn't be any foolishness about beatnik-type electives. Accounting, that was the deal. Accounting, and nothing but. His father was into a lot of things—

real estate development, part owner of a furniture store, silent partner in two car dealerships—and if there was anyone he respected, it was a sharp CPA.

Up ahead Marvin could see the long jetty that protected the entrance to Mission Bay. A sailboat was working its way through the channel, bright red-and-green navigational lights atop its mast. Would it have been so awful to be a CPA? Marvin wondered. Would that have been such a terrible fate?

He'd kept his nose clean until he was almost done with his sophomore year. His grades were average, and had he not spent so much study time idly sketching on the big charcoal pad he had to keep hidden whenever he left home each morning he might've even made Dean's List. But no. He had kept going over to the Mandeville Art Center, looking with painful longing at the pictures and sculptures in the student gallery, peeking into the classrooms that were full of paint-splattered easels and reeked of the intoxicating aroma of oils and turpentine. Sometimes there would be a model in the classroom, a young man or woman atop a pedestal, posing for the students. At other times, the students worked on their own projects, canvases with still lifes and portraits and bright abstracts.

Surely one little course wouldn't do any harm. His father might even overlook it. After all, it wasn't as if he were giving up accounting; he *was* required to take a certain number of electives, anyway. . . .

But notice it he did, and the scene that followed was terrible indeed; all the more so because Marvin stood his ground and shouted back at his father, making all kinds of statements about how it was his life and he could do whatever the hell he wanted. His mother wept in the background, half sprawled on the sofa and crying as if the world had come to an end. His father had laughed in that harsh

57

way of his and said, Big man, are you? Well, you can get the hell out of here and support your own lazy butt, *big man*. When I was your age I was in a goddamn *cement factory* busting my ass for a *buck and a quarter* an hour and—

The people at the student employment office were nice, but the job bussing tables at the Commons Cafeteria wasn't quite enough to cover classes and one-third of the rent in the off-campus rat trap he shared with two other guys. So at night he took a bus across town to work from midnight to four at the farmer's market, minimum wage, six nights a week. He had to drop his class load from fifteen hours to ten . . . but things just didn't work out. He found it difficult to pay attention in class, even if it *was* a class in art appreciation. . . .

He went downtown and visited the Armed Forces recruiting center. The recruiter was a chief machinist's mate with submariner's dolphins pinned above three rows of ribbons. Marvin asked about the programs that offered something in the way of college assistance. The recruiter spoke soothingly, using a gentle tone that belied his sinewy bulk, telling him that there were plenty of opportunities to earn college credits while on active duty, and further down the pike, when he became a veteran, there would be plenty of financial assistance. It was a smooth pitch, and Marvin enjoyed listening to it. He thought about how good it would be to have the pressure off, to let the military take care of his feeding and housing. His eyes kept flickering to a framed poster hanging in the office. It showed a sharp-looking guy in sailor's blues, standing inside a destroyer's pilothouse and looking out at a South Sea village.

He went to boot camp two weeks later, right in San Diego. And was discharged a few months later "Under Other Than Honorable Conditions." Not as bad as a Dishonorable Discharge, or even a Bad Conduct Discharge. But it wasn't exactly the honorable kind, either.

Marvin reached the end of his walk. It was called Yogi Beach, a little bit of land at the mouth of the San Diego River Floodway, right next to the Mission Bay Channel jetty. He looked back toward Ocean Beach, where cars were moving slowly along the beachfront road, silhouetted against the lights of stores and houses and apartment buildings. The beach itself seemed unpopulated, but he counted four bonfires in the barbecue pits now, wavering like distant beacons. He took a macrobiotic cupcake from the sack and started to eat without appetite.

The less-than-honorable discharge had been the worst part about getting kicked out of the Navy. As more than one potential employer had told him, there's plenty of guys who didn't screw up in the service who're looking for work, too. The cupcake had broken into dry little components, crumbling in his mouth like inedible dirt clods. He chewed listlessly and cared not at all when crumbs fell from his mouth. He peeled off the plastic top of the carrot juice. It was sweet and pulpy, and it made him grimace.

The discharge had closed a lot of doors, all right. All except for Hattstaedt's Sup'r Serv. Good old Mr. Sam had given him a break. Had even lent him some money to get the apartment at the Cota Arms.

It seemed impossible, but he was nearing the second anniversary of his stay at Hattstaedt's. Two whole years. Each day of which had seemed interminable, but the sum had gone by in a snap of the fingers. Two fucking *years*.

He'd had his twenty-fourth birthday a month ago. No one had noticed. Twenty-four damn years old. Once that had seemed like an advanced age. Now it just seemed like time was speeding up, going by like one of those fast-motion films that show clouds hurtling overhead and the sun careening through the sky . . . or a hand growing loose and gnarled as it held tight on the trigger of a gas pump's nozzle.

He began trudging back, cutting across the beach, heading directly for town. He came within thirty yards of one of the bonfires, close enough to hear someone strumming a guitar. But his path only cut that close because he was heading for one of the municipal trash cans, into which he threw the remains of his dinner.

Marvin finished the last of the six-pack and tossed the can in the Alpha Beta grocery bag that served as his wastebasket. He listened to Johnny Carson tell another joke, then got up as the audience roared. He swayed a little before he caught himself, then headed toward the bathroom.

He felt as if he were walking on stilts, going faster than he wanted. Well, he'd set out to get a little drunk, and there was surely no need for the other six-pack now. He relieved himself and started brushing his teeth, using too much toothpaste and jamming the brush into his mouth with exaggerated strokes.

Then he froze, staring at himself in the mirror, toothbrush in mouth, a ribbon of spittle trailing down to the sink. There was another roar of TV laughter, the Gold Star's tiny speaker making it sound weird and distorted.

Boy, you have really gone over the limit this time, because for a moment there it seemed that there was something wrong with the mirror, like it'd gotten a little bit out of synch, because I swear to God when you were brushing your right molars, it was brushing—

Marvin laughed, toothbrush still in his mouth. Synchronization problems courtesy of Miller High Life. He rinsed out his mouth and hit the light, turned off the TV, and went to bed.

From faraway he heard a record player turned way up. Vintage Earth, Wind & Fire. Marvin put his hands behind his head.

Of course it was just the beers. . . .

He sailed through the night effortlessly, arms outstretched, balmy air making his hair flutter around his head. It was wonderfully serene . . . and he was full of boundless strength, infinite power. He rolled lazily, laughing, thinking of a pastel he'd seen at an art gallery, one of those Chagalls, something about a man grown impossibly huge and elongated, floating above his village.

He let the wind carry him where it would, the lights below a galaxy of jewels far more alluring than the stars above. He made out the familiar landmarks, the tall downtown buildings, an abandoned amusement park, a full-to-overflowing yacht basin. He could even pinpoint the intersection where Hattstaedt's Sup'r Serv stood, and a little stab of anger flickered through his serenity. He floated onward, to the northeast, and he sensed that he was . . . going down a little bit, losing altitude.

He didn't like this part. He didn't want to come down. But he didn't know how to get himself back up.

He saw that he was heading straight for a big modernistic building, set by itself on a grassy hill. His new trajectory would splatter him against the building's wall, and he was seized with a cold panic.

He picked up speed rapidly. The silken caress of the night changed to a harsh, tearing wind, filling his ears with a roar. He rolled up in a little ball and began tumbling. He heard the distant sounds of traffic as he passed over the eight lanes of Interstate 5. He knew the impact would come at any moment. . . .

But the roaring ceased, the tumbling stopped, and he saw that he was in an empty stairwell of some sort, hanging a few feet above the landing. And whatever had empowered him to fly suddenly took its leave, for he dropped down hard, barking his still-tender knee. The pain was sharp and hot, and he cried out.

The stairwell's fluorescent lighting cast huge double shadows against the cinderblock walls. He had no idea where he was, but he loathed the place. Massaging his knee, all he could think of was that a moment ago he'd been high above the world, as happy and uncaring as a cloud. Now this!

He used the steel railing to slowly pull himself to a standing position and began working his way down the stairs, grimacing each time the bruised knee took weight. The only sound was the hum of the fluorescents, magnified by the empty stairwell. He cursed each step, cursed the building, cursed the providence that had brought him here.

He finally made it to the landing. There was a heavy steel door with a small wire-mesh window, stenciled over with a number five. He looked through the window and saw a long carpeted corridor with doors to either side. It could have been the interior of a high-rise Howard Johnson's, but it wasn't. At the far end of the corridor was the corner of a nurses' station, and leaning against it was a trim young brunette in uniform, writing on a metal clipboard.

The pain in his knee ebbed away, forgotten.

You know where you are now, don't you?

It wasn't a thought. It was a voice, like a whisper from a dark alleyway.

And you know who's here waiting for you, don't you, boy? All wrapped up, and ready to go. . . .

Marvin smiled, but it was cold and shadowy, like a winter's twilight.

The nurse looked at her wristwatch. She snapped the clipboard closed and walked out of sight, down an adjoining corridor. Marvin pushed the door open wide. There was a low-grade institutional hum, but otherwise it was quiet.

He began to walk slowly, without hurry.

You admired her beauty above all others. Was humbly grateful for whatever crumb of attention she'd toss your way. Worked over and over on the only portrait that had ever meant anything to you, never satisfied with a line that did not approach her perfection.

He reached the door and pushed it open. The only illumination was a nightlight by her bed. He walked forward softly, almost on tiptoe, eyes wide in the darkened room. Her head was turned sideways, her red hair dark against the pillow, her chest barely moving with the rhythmic exhalations of sleep.

And when she had needed help most, who had protected her? And for what? What?

He reached out . . .

She shifted and turned, and her eyes opened wide, moisture glistening against the irises.

He slipped into bed quickly and silently, and when she pushed against him and tried to scream it was like the rustling of a tiny bird, so easy to subdue, so easy to force her legs apart, so easy to press himself against her, like some great crushing machine squeezing down on a junked car, making the thin-gauge steel crinkle and snap.

□

F I V E

"Well, I'm surprised to see you this morning." Mr. Sam had a Salem between his lips, which bobbed up and down as he spoke. "Thought for sure that pissant sergeant would've had you signing confessions for the last eight or nine murders they got on the books."

"It was nothing." Marvin shrugged. "Just a mistake."

Mr. Sam held Marvin's eyes for a moment. There was something different about the boy, but not like yesterday, when he had had that killing look in his eyes.

The service bell dinged, and it hurt Mr. Sam's ears. He'd slugged back an entire fifth of Four Roses last night, after he'd woken thinking about old Corporal Embry. Lord, but did he feel ornery today.

"I'd better go take care of the customer."

"Yeah, well, just remember I got my eye on you, Moy. Dangerous fella like you gets me so nervous I just might end up wetting my pants."

Mr. Sam walked away hacking and wheezing, which for him was what passed for laughter, although not at its usual volume.

Marvin walked over to a shiny new Supra at the full-serve. It was strange, but he was actually eager to begin work this morning. What was stranger was that the six-pack hadn't left him with a trace of hangover. He felt just fine and dandy.

Dell and J.J. came on duty at two, heading straight for an old Chrysler Imperial that the owner said was rattling at the front end. It was sitting on the lift's saddle, and J.J. got the hydraulics going while Dell took down a hand lamp from the overhead pulley. It took Dell all of twenty seconds to discover the problem. The casing that held the transmission in against the mounting bracket was cracked. It was only hairline now, but it surely wasn't going to get any better.

Although Dell hadn't done any welding in this particular shop, he'd seen a banged-up arc welder in a corner of the storeroom, a Hobart, if he remembered right. He told J.J. to get it, and to see if there was any protective gear, too.

Dell studied the job, trying to figure the best way to go. He felt where the crack ran to the top of the transmission and realized it was all but inaccessible. An ordinary mechanic would've just unbolted the whole goddamn thing and laid it out on a workbench, but Dell considered himself something more than ordinary. Not that he gave a flying Dutchman's fuck what Mr. Sam or the Imperial's owner or anybody else on this planet thought about him; it was just that when it came to machinery, you were under a sort of obligation to do the job the best way you knew how.

J.J. wheeled out the transformer and Dell set about the business of getting the job ready. He went slow, teaching J.J. as he went. *Real* slow. Dell thought the Chicano's usual dog-earnest look was slightly fuzzed and red-eyed today, as if he'd gone to the Sterno after the Thunderbird had run dry.

It was while he was showing J.J. how to set the voltage that Mr. Sam came into the bay. He was on his way to check the GMC compact pickup in the other bay when he saw the welding gear. He stopped, surprised. Then his eyes narrowed.

"I didn't give nobody no permission to break out all this shit."

The mechanic looked up. *"Permission?"*

"This gear ain't any goddamn toy." Mr. Sam took two steps toward the Imperial and yanked off the ground clamp. He pointed it at Dell. "You done any stick arc before?"

The barrel-chested biker took his time standing up, and on purpose. Experience had taught him that at times like these, when he found himself getting excited, he'd ought to take things slow. "Who the fuck hasn't?"

"Pretty smart boy, ain't you? Just tell me what you were fixing to do with it."

Dell showed him the crack wordlessly. Mr. Sam snorted. "Welding the underside's going to be easy, sure. But how about the top? Going to have to pull the whole damn transmission. This here job's going to take the both of you all day—and I gave the owner a written estimate of no more than four hundred dollars, labor and all."

"I'll just hold a mirror up in there, see what I'm doing."

"A mirror, huh? Just like that."

"Try working on a bike sometime. Makes this feel like the Grand Canyon."

"Just don't take too fucking long." He turned his back and walked away, tossing the ground clamp aside.

Dell sighed as he picked it up. More and more of late he was getting a little bitty urge to lay a tire iron upside the bossman's head. And urges like that meant it was time to pull stakes and hit that lonesome road.

He reset the ground. "Nice guy, eh? Sure grateful about getting four hundred bucks for a job that'll cost one welding rod and twenty minutes of labor."

J.J. shrugged. "You get half, man."

"Yeah. Two hundred bucks for twenty minutes' work." He tied on the leather apron. "Real money."

J.J. grinned. "Sounds real enough to me."

Dell worked his hands into the heavy duty gloves, which were a little too small. "Man, all around you are ways to make *real* money. Even right here at this roach trap there's . . . aw, you wouldn't be interested."

Dell put on the helmet, but out of the corner of his eye he noticed that J.J. had taken an alert, wary interest.

"That's right, man," J.J. said, "I wouldn't be interested."

Dell slipped a rod in the stinger. "Suit yourself. Stand back, and don't look at the arc."

J.J. backed off, a pained expression on his face. The fourteen months he'd spent at Chino were the worst of his life. No way he would risk going back to that hellhole. No way at *all*.

There was a harsh crackling noise as sparks poured from underneath the Imperial.

Marvin jogged on the sidewalk at an easy clip, thoroughly enjoying himself. The exercise was sharpening him up and lifting his spirits—and he knew that tonight would be one of the good nights at the easel, the kind where every stroke would be unhesitant, and the world of work and worry would fade into utter meaninglessness.

He took a right on Santa Monica, heading straight for the beach. It was one of the run-down areas, and a scarecrow of an old man asked for a quarter as Marvin jogged by. He made it to the big parking lot near the lifeguard station and slowed to a wide-gaited walk before hitting the beach.

There was the usual late-afternoon late-summer crowd, teeny-boppers in garish bikinis, old couples with pants legs rolled up, college-age people at the volleyball nets. Marvin was about forty yards from one of the nets when a ball came sailing his way, hit the sand, and rolled directly in front of him.

"Hey!" A girl detached herself from the group and came trotting his way, breasts wobbling behind her microscopic bikini top. "Little help, please!"

Marvin smiled as he picked up the ball. Just another summertime jock glad to lend a hand to your typical beach bun, painfully lovely category. He started to toss it back, then thought it'd be more impressive to make it really fly. Use a real volleyball serve, smack it the hell over there. He tossed the ball up and brought his fist along in a wide, swinging arc . . . but his timing was just a hair off, and the ball smacked against his wrist. It careened off to the side, sailing even farther from the girl.

There were groans from the volleyballers. One of the boys scampered after the still-bouncing ball. The bikinied one cupped her hands and yelled, *"Thanks loads, dipshit!"* The husky young man behind her doubled over laughing, teeth white against his perfect tan.

Marvin's embarrassment was as sharp as a blade, and he worked his mouth without making a sound, wondering if it would do any good to shout an apology. But the bikinied girl was already walking back to her friends with angry strides, and the moment was gone. Marvin turned and headed toward the surf, massaging his stinging wrist.

The wave action was heavier than usual, cresting at three to five feet before rolling over and smashing down into a hard rolling spray. Marvin started walking north, keeping just above the waves' uprush. The planned jog was totally forgotten; he was consumed with a desperate, private litany that ran through his mind with metronomic intensity:

Nothing ever goes right, not ever. Just when you start to get up, you always get slapped down. You're always going to be a fuckup. It's never going to get better.

A middle-aged jogger in a color-coordinated outfit came up from behind and passed on ahead, pounding along at a clip that was as heavy and ponderous as a water buffalo's, the little wires to his stereo headset bouncing in cadence. A couple was walking toward Marvin slowly, arm in arm and heads bowed together, looking as crisply romantic as an advertisement for breath mints. They passed on to the south. Marvin saw a slender woman just ahead, shuffling toward him, totally absorbed with something in her hands. As she came nearer he saw that it was some sort of seashell, then she looked up and there was a moment of startled recognition.

"Oh, hello there." It was Miss Ontiveros, the Cota Arms' manager. Her smile was brief and formal, but she made no move to continue on.

"Hi." Marvin's heart thumped. He started to put his hands

in his pockets, but there were none on the jogging shorts. He tried to make the awkward move blend into thrusting his hands on his hips. "Out for a walk?" And he thought, of course she is, what else would she be doing here?

Kathryn nodded, and the smile reappeared for a brief moment. Strands of brown hair battered at her face. "Just feeling kind of restless, you know. . . ."

Marvin nodded eagerly.

She looked at the shell she'd been carrying, then tossed it away. "Listen," she said slowly, wiping her hands, "I was just heading down to the fishing pier. Why don't you come with me? I'd really like some company just now."

Marvin was silent with astonishment. Would he like to go walking with her? Christ . . . "Sure." He tried to sound casual. "That'd be great."

They started walking south, toward the big municipal pier. It seemed incredible to Marvin that she'd just come out and ask him to go with her, just like that, as if it were the most natural thing in the world.

"Really nice afternoon, isn't it Miss Ontiveros?"

She smiled. "Kathryn, remember?"

"Right, sorry." He grinned happily. "Nice afternoon, isn't it, Kathryn?"

She looked at him and this time the smile was also in her eyes, and Marvin was surprised at how it thrilled him. But then her beguiling sparkle disappeared as suddenly as it came, and she turned her attention back to the sand in front of her, walking with her arms folded, long brown hair hiding her profile.

Marvin was desperate to find something to talk about, and he resorted to a brief description of a movie he'd recently seen. Kathryn made appropriate sounds of polite interest, and it finally dawned on Marvin that she might

70

prefer no talk at all, so he let the conversation lapse and soon found that it was more comfortable, too.

They went up the concrete staircase, then began walking on the weathered boards. The pier, a quarter-mile in length, seemed to stretch before them endlessly. There were late-afternoon strollers and joggers, and fishermen with lines cast over the railing. They walked the entire length without saying a word, and when they reached the end they leaned on the railing together. Seagulls floated overhead, holding into the breeze motionlessly. The sun lay on the horizon.

Marvin savored the moment. It was nice being with someone, even if it was someone he hardly knew. It made the incident with the volleyball players . . . well, why not forget about it altogether? He stole a quick glance at his companion. Her elbows were resting on the wooden railing, her hands clasped, and the warm breeze played with strands of her hair. She stared at her thumbnails with intense concentration, her mouth pulled down at the corners.

Marvin looked back out over the Pacific. If Kathryn wanted to be quiet, that was fine with him. Her mere presence was enough. He studied the outline of a ship on the horizon, some kind of naval vessel, and he guessed that it was one of those Spruance-class destroyers.

But the spirit of Kathryn Ontiveros was not so serene. She was so deep in thought she'd almost forgotten about Marvin, although at first she'd thought his company—anyone's company—would have been welcome. But nothing seemed capable of blotting out a little incident that had occurred two weeks ago, an incident she kept telling herself was trivial and insignificant in the extreme.

But it just wouldn't let go. It kept coming at her like some kind of homely and earnest suitor, shadowing her as she went about her day.

How she wished she hadn't gone to that stupid party at the Geralds'. Then she wouldn't have met that boy, that surfer or lifeguard or whatever the hell he was. And so *young*—God! Whatever had been on her mind?

She looked past her thumbnails, down to where a fishing line trailed in the water.

Getting down and boogying, that's what had been on her mind. A little cutting up and cutting loose—all nicely oiled by the Geralds' generous supply of second-rate booze and first-rate dope, thanks ever so much. And a true Valhalla of partydom it had been, the Bauhaus condo jammed to overflowing with taut, tanned bodies, huge speakers pounding out enough decibels to register on the Ricther scale, ground-floor doors thrown wide to the beach and whatever nighttime passerby might care to join in.

In fact, the boy she'd met might have strayed off the beach himself, but that was hardly important when someone with such a great pair of shoulders turns out to be unexpectedly funny, and even kind of sweet . . . altogether, just the companion for a night when the coke is good enough to get you floating a few feet off the carpet and the music powerful enough to jump your pulse to triathalon levels.

She ended up taking him back to her Cota Arms apartment. It wasn't something she often did, but what better capper for a wonderfully gonzo party than a little no-holds-barred roll in the hay with a total stranger?

The young man's performance turned out to be relentless if unsophisticated, and that was fine at first, but as the night wore on and the booze and dope lost their hold, things became as sweaty and strenuous as an all-day session at the aerobics studio. Exhaustion eventually overcame her, and she pliantly let herself be maneuvered into yet another position for the endless, insatiable hammering. But somehow it finally ended, and Kathryn tumbled into sleep as if she had been pushed over the lip of the Grand Canyon.

There hadn't been any time to pull the drapes, and so the harsh morning light woke her before she was fully rested. She padded into the kitchenette feeling creaky and worn and sour, and more than a little irritated that she still had to go through the rigamarole of giving Schwarzenegger Junior his complimentary breakfast before she could show him the door. But her spirits improved as she went through the familiar motions of squeezing oranges and cracking eggs, and suddenly he was there hugging her from behind, all charm and sweetness and warm muscle. They started laughing and horsing around, and the sour morning changed to something full of promise, and just when Kathryn was thinking that he wasn't such a bad sort after all, the boy suddenly let go and stared at her with shock, as if he'd just caught on to something he should've understood long ago, and then without the least hint of guile or malice, said, *Hey, you're really old.*

The eggs began to pop and sizzle in the big cast-iron skillet. The bright morning light filled the kitchenette with a clean, flat intensity. The kid's simple face creased with worry as he became dimly aware that he had somehow blundered, and he announced, *No offense lady, I mean, hey, you got a really great bod and everything, but—*

She was remote and polite, but it seemed to take forever to get him out the door, all the while telling herself that she'd wasted enough time with this surfer idiot and had to get on with her day.

She set about a vigorous housecleaning, a top to bottom on-your-knees scrubfest, everything out of the cabinets, everything neatly rearranged, windows cleaned inside and out, all books back in the bookshelves, dust banged out of the throw rugs, closet cleaned and reorganized with left-overs thrown in a pile for the Salvation Army, bathroom walls scrubbed with double-strength Lysol. . . .

It was in the bathroom that she suddenly lost steam. She was on her knees in front of the cabinet under the sink, bringing order to the mass of bottles and vials and rolls of toilet paper, when she came upon the thing she'd bought at Ralph's only last week, still in its bright rectangular box, plastic wrapping intact. *Washes Away Only the Gray*, the let-ters proclaimed in dainty, feminine script. *It's as easy as shampooing your hair!*

She stared at it blankly, as if confronted by a nonsensical artifact of a forgotten civilization. But the words on the box made sense, all right. Too much sense.

She closed her eyes and told herself that thirty-eight was a fine age to be, just fine. She was in her prime, thoroughly enjoying herself, and nothing was wrong at all, at all. Buy-ing a little hair goop was just . . . was just, well . . .

Maybe she'd been in Ocean Beach too long. She had only planned on being here . . . what? One year? Two at the outside? Whatever—it was only supposed to have been a rest stop, a place for a troubled young woman to kick back and get her head together before continuing on with the great adventure that was to be her life. And after the tumult of the previous years, it was exactly what she needed, like slipping into a great, warm bath. The weather was invariably temperate, the people undemanding, and stim-ulation (whenever required . . . and of whatever sort) was as readily available as the fruit on the perpetually-blooming trees.

Hey, you're really—

She had only been twenty-five when she arrived. Plenty

of time yet—hell, *acres* of time yet—to do whatever she wanted. And time had become as slow and unnoticeable as the growth of a garden—no movement at all, if you sat down and watched it. But leave it alone for a bit, and then come back and have the breath knocked from your lungs when you see that it's become a goddamn *jungle*.

I mean, no offense lady, but—

Ocean Beach wasn't a way station anymore—not after thirteen years. Who was she kidding? Ocean Beach was *it*.

"Kathryn?" Marvin's face was twisted with worry. "Are you okay?" He didn't know what to think. He'd been so wrapped up in the view that he hadn't noticed anything was wrong until the woman bent her head to her hands and began shuddering. He reached out to soothe her, to touch her and pat her, but his hand wavered a few inches above her back. He pulled away.

"Kathryn, you all right?"

She straightened up slowly, nodding but not speaking. She brushed some of her hair out of the way. "Yeah, sure. Come on, let's go."

They turned and walked down the pier. It was a silent walk. Dusk was surrendering to dark, but die-hard surfers were still hard at it, black shapes against whitely-cresting waves.

Had they not lived in the same complex, she would have said good-bye as soon as she could. As it was she endured the silent walk, but when they came upon Cota Arms she found she didn't want to say good-bye after all. There was something about Marvin that she found sweetly appealing. It was rare to meet a man who was genuinely shy these days, much less one that had any sort of real talent.

"Thanks for putting up with me, Marvin. It was nice not to walk around alone for a change."

"Huh? Oh, sure. Anytime."

"Listen, I'd ask you in for a sandwich, but I have to teach a class tonight. Would you like to drop by tomorrow?"

Kathryn smiled when she saw his face go a little red. "Ah, ah, yeah, of course. That would be great."

"Seven?"

"Seven's fine. Whatever you say."

S I X

"Good afternoon, Sergeant Perry. I'm Dr. Simon. Sorry to have kept you waiting so long."

Perry wouldn't have bet on it, but he wore his most diplomatic smile as he shook the young doctor's hand. "That's all right. Where's Dr. Franklin?"

Simon had fine blond hair that, though closely cropped, managed to look disheveled. His goatee, on the other hand, was full and luxuriant. "He's no longer in charge of the case, not since her specific malady was identified."

"Which is?"

"Well, let's just say that physically she's fine."

Let's just say she's nuts, Perry thought. "I see."

"Actually, Sergeant, I'm rather glad that you came by today; there're some questions I'd like to ask."

"Oh?" Perry's guard went up. He had never liked shrinks, and the sessions he'd had with the police psychiatrist hadn't done anything to increase his respect for that voodoo branch of science. "What about?"

"Please." The fifth floor had a small waiting room, and the doctor indicated the heavy sofa.

"I'm comfortable standing, thanks."

"Oh. Well, then. I understand that Miss Collier had a severe reaction when she was confronted by her attacker."

Perry shook his head vigorously. "No way."

"But Dr. Franklin said—"

"Oh, she went berserk when she saw the suspect, all right. But he turned out not to be the perpetrator after all."

Dr. Simon frowned. "Really."

"Yeah. The boy has witnesses who put him somewhere else at the time of the assault."

"Hmmm, well . . . perhaps he bore some similarity . . ."

"Perhaps. But tell me, Doctor, what exactly is Miss Collier's condition?"

"Well, initially I thought it was entirely due to the trauma of the assault, which is not uncommon in certain personalities. But I'm beginning to suspect that the psychosis is deeply rooted, only just now coming to the surface."

"Psychosis, huh?" Perry undid the wrapper on a piece of Wrigley's Spearmint. "Has she had trouble like this in the past?"

"That's just the thing. I've talked with her family physician and reviewed her records, and her history has been

78

perfectly normal, except for a broken arm when she was eleven from a skateboard accident. Still, that doesn't necessarily mean . . ." The doctor tugged at his beard, lost in thought.

Yeah, Perry thought, in the world of shrinkdom, up means down, nothing means something, and everyone's drooling over their parents' private parts. "Doctor, would it be possible for me to see Miss Collier for a few minutes?"

"Hmm, what?"

"I'd like to see your patient, please."

"Why? I can tell you right now that anything she might say in the course of an . . . official investigation will be completely unreliable."

"I don't really want to interview her, Doctor. I'd just like to get my own idea of her condition. It has to go in my report."

"Well . . ." Dr. Simon glanced at his wristwatch. "She should be awake now. Very well, you can look in on her if it's only for a few moments. Follow me, please."

They headed down the carpeted hallway and went into a different wing than the one Genevieve had been in earlier. Perry was surprised to feel butterflies in his stomach—crazy people gave him the creeps; always had, ever since he was a rookie. There was something about them that was worse than your standard crook. It was like they were some kind of flesh-and-blood robot, with no human at the controls.

Dr. Simon pushed open an unmarked door and Perry followed him inside. Genevieve lay in the room's only bed, bathed in sunlight and looking out the window. She did not turn to greet her visitors.

"Miss Collier?" Dr. Simon called softly. "Genevieve? It's me."

She continued to stare at the four lanes of Genesee Avenue, which wound its way between scrub-dotted hills into an area of small modern office buildings.

"Genevieve, someone's come here especially to see you today. He'd like to talk with you a moment, if you feel up to it."

Still she did not turn. Perry noted that her red hair was not as resplendent as it had looked when he first entered the room. The rich sunlight, which made the white bed-sheets fairly glow, had tricked him into thinking it was lustrous. Looking at it now, he was reminded of the brittle alkali scrub in the desert, parched and stiff and lifeless.

"Well, Genevieve, if you don't feel like talking to-day . . ."

Perry touched the younger man's arm. "May I try?" he whispered.

The doctor looked at Perry with irritation, then sighed. "Go ahead."

"Genevieve?" Perry stepped closer to the bed. "Gene-vieve, it's me, Sergeant Perry. Remember?"

No response. Perry realized that she'd lost some weight. Quite a bit, in fact. Her arms seemed as thin as cornstalks. "Genevieve . . . can you tell me what it is you're looking at?"

A big flatbed was working its way up Genesee, black smoke pouring from the twin exhausts behind the cab.

"Night," Genevieve said quietly.

Perry and Dr. Simon exchanged glances.

"Night?" Perry asked.

She turned her head slowly. Her cheeks were stained with tears. Auschwitz, Perry thought. She looks as if she came out of fucking Auschwitz.

"I'm waiting for the night." Her face was a pitiful cari-cature of what it had once been, but the worst of it was her

80

eyes. They shone out of her dissipated face like a pair of flashlights, the deep green of her irises spangled with hard, glittering diamonds. Crazy, Perry thought. So crazy you didn't know if she was crying sad or crying happy.

"Is that why you're crying, honey?"

She nodded, sniffling.

"Tell me about the night."

"When it's dark," she said in a little girl's voice, "he comes to me."

Professor Albert Willings wandered the darkened parking lot for some minutes before he found his metallic gray BMW, and when he did he let out a happy sigh. But even that slight movement made his eyes water, and he touched his jaw as he waited for the pain to subside.

It had been wired shut, with only a sixteenth of an inch play. There didn't seem to be much else the hospital could do, and still they refused to discharge him. Had to put his foot down with that pug-faced nurse, telling her he'd be damned if he'd spend another interminable night listening to his roommate's wretched moans. Even had to get a little nasty with that young doctor, but Professor Willings got his way in the end, as he knew he would.

He got in the car and spent some moments adjusting the seat, irritated at the inconvenience. One of his teaching assistants had brought the car round earlier in the day— Barbara Ann, tall of stature and buck of tooth. Actually *cried* when she came to his room, saying how horrible it was that he'd been so savagely brutalized. Professor Willings squirmed uncomfortably while the homely girl wept. It reminded him of the first time she had carried on, blubbering like some tiresome child as she lay in the tangle of his queen-size bed.

Barbara Ann volunteered to drive him home. Said she

would wait however long was necessary for him to be discharged. But fortunately the girl had left before he woke from his nap, and the keys were on the nightstand.

He twisted the ignition, and the well-tuned engine immediately purred into life. It was no longer under warranty, but he kept to the recommended maintenance schedule with a fervor that would have pleased a German automotive engineer. He turned on the radio, and the passenger compartment filled with the soft modulations of a lone cello—he was pleased that Barbara Ann hadn't changed channels or volume.

Professor Willings pulled out of the parking lot and drove down the hospital's winding access road. His headlights swung over a tall man standing near the stop sign by the main road, thumb outstretched. Professor Willings looked away—hitchhikers irritated him. Of course, it was different when he was young—during his sophomore year at NYCC he had thumbed his way all the way from New York to Florida—but now there was so much viciousness in this sorry world it was only prudent that roaming vagrants be locked up.

There wasn't any traffic, and he stepped on the gas. The engine accelerated smoothly, and when the turbo kicked in Professor Willings felt a small twinge of pleasure. The entrance ramp for the interstate came up quickly, and he took it with a sporty twist of the wheel, wishing again that he'd gone with the stick shift. He pulled into the sparse traffic of the southbound lanes and settled down for the forty-minute drive.

Professor Willings enjoyed being back in his car. It felt as snug and secure as the inside of a well-engineered womb—especially at night, with just the muted glow of the instrument lights, and a stereo system that was better than the one at home.

The BMW was the one thing in his life that was exactly as he wanted it to be. Now if he were only driving to a *home* that was as he wanted—that would be truly lovely. *But, no*, Professor Willings told himself grimly. Dear Andrea and that grotesque lawyer had gutted him like some kind of game fish at the divorce proceedings, making sure the best he could ever hope for was some second-rate condo out in the sticks. And a *rented* one at that. . . .

He grimaced, and it made the wires in the back of his jaw come alive. He forced himself to relax, concentrating on the road, and presently the needling pain lapsed into the throbbing ache that he could almost ignore.

But, oh God, how he'd make sure that . . . that *boy* would feel pain! Professor Willings tightened his hands on the wheel, simmering, imagining how the hoodlum would try to make himself smaller in the courtroom when that happy day arrived. And then the satisfaction of watching him sentenced to one of those state-run hellholes, there no doubt to be brutally sodomized each and every day. But of course that wouldn't be the end of it—Professor Willings had already decided to file a civil lawsuit of monumental proportions. Sue the boy right into the ground. And so what if he could never pay it off? That wasn't the point. The point was to make sure the consequences of his actions would dog him the rest of his days, with U.S. marshalls banging at whatever door he lived at in the country, seizing whatever small sums he managed to accumulate, until the boy had no alternative but to jump off a—

The radio's music changed tone abruptly. The bow drew across the cello's strings harshly, bringing the melody down into some kind of discordant angst. Professor Willings was surprised—he hadn't thought it'd been a modern piece. He tried listening to it, but it only reminded him of the pain in his jaw. It even made him a little bit nervous . . . and Professor Willings found himself checking the rearview mirror, then sweeping the instrument gauges for a sign of something amiss.

He turned off the weird, irritating music. A car loomed brightly in the rearview mirror, then passed on ahead.

Professor Willings was sure the police would find that vicious animal, whoever he was. That sergeant seemed like a competent fellow—perhaps even a shade *too* competent. Asked some rather odd questions about what had been going on in his office immediately prior to the attack, questions which the professor had fended off as tactfully as possible. After all, Genevieve had to be protected. The sergeant just didn't know how it was, the way these young girls would get so terribly infatuated with their profess—

He felt warmth against his neck, like a breath.

Professor Willings glanced in the rearview mirror, alarmed . . . but nothing was there. Of course. He wiped at his neck, frowning.

He would take a long bath when he got home. Perhaps even fix up a batch of lime daiquiris. Why not? He didn't have to work tomorrow. And he sure as hell was restricted to a liquid diet for the next . . .

He checked the mirror again. But it only showed distant headlights, some pairs gaining, some receding, others holding steady.

Professor Willings found himself thinking about a story he'd read in last week's paper, something about a woman who'd been attacked in her car. Left her doors unlocked when she went into a shopping mall, and the fellow just slipped in and waited on the floor of the backseat.

It was something you hear about from time to time, but lord, what a horror it must have been! He always locked his doors, of course. And sometimes even glanced in the

84

backseat before getting in. But this time . . . come to think of it . . . that stupid little teaching assistant . . .

He glanced at the mirror again.

Nothing.

He craned his neck forward, changing his viewing angle into the mirror so that he could peer down into the void of the backseat.

Empty.

Professor Willings settled back into the seat, swallowing thickly. The whispering of the road was oppressive, maddening in its sameness. He turned the radio back on, but the cello was still in the midst of agonized tonalities, and he clicked the preset channel buttons until the speakers filled with the soft, generic melody of a Muzak station. He passed his hand across his mouth.

Yes, a *big* batch of daiquiris would be in order . . . he thought of how good they would taste, how perfect a counterpoint to the steaming bath. And who knew? He might even give Barbara Ann a call (surely she would recognize his grunt). The girl had almost learned how to give a decent massage. . . .

His mind dragged back to the story in the paper. He wondered about the particulars of the incident. Had it happened during the day? Or late at night? How far had the woman driven before the intruder made his presence known?

Professor Willings turned his head sharply, trying to look down into the floor of the backseat. The pain in his jaw flared up mightily, and he gave a little cry through his clenched teeth. . . .

He turned around, blinded by the pain. He gripped the wheel tightly, holding the middle of the lane as best he could. It was agony, it was terrible, but at least he'd seen enough to know that he was alone, that he was *sure* no one was hiding back there. . . .

85

Unless, of course, the intruder was in dark clothes, pressed against the shadows.

Professor Willings took a hand from the wheel and rubbed his jaw. *All right,* he told himself, *Enough already—no one's in the goddamn backseat.* Surely he would've sensed the intruder's presence shortly after climbing in. A hundred little clues would have let him know—breathing, body heat . . . Christ, *thousands* of things. They say a blind person can walk in a room and know that someone's there. Even a sighted person knows when a stranger's in their house. It isn't some supernatural ability. It isn't any—

God, how had it been? Had the woman just looked into the mirror and seen him there, grinning like some nightmare jack-in-the-box? Or had it been quick—a hand suddenly wrapped around her throat, his thick, moist giggling close against her ear?

Professor Willings put his foot on the power brakes and pressed hard. A pair of headlights in the rearview mirror grew frighteningly bright, and the fast-closing car swerved into the next lane as its horn blasted on a long, receding note.

The professor gripped the wheel tightly, part of his mind telling him that whoever was in the backseat would be trying to get up now, alarmed at the sudden change. He increased pressure on the brake pedal, and there was a loud, agonized squeal. He prayed that the sudden deceleration would keep the intruder pinned to the floor.

The BMW trundled onto the shoulder.

Professor Willings had the door open before the car was fully stopped, and he punched the seatbelt release and scrambled from the car frantically, as if the passenger compartment had come alive with a swarm of hornets. He stumbled from the car and tried to run—a long, loose-gaited, out-of-balance sprint, but he sprawled to his hands and knees.

Air whistled into his clamped jaw painfully, and he gasped and cried as he waited for his pursuer's hands to clamp down on his neck. . . .

But nothing happened.

He looked around. Cars roared perilously near, loud as a parade of heavy tanks in Red Square, buffeting him with warm gusts of night air. No one was in the BMW, or standing nearby. He got up slowly, wiping his hands, completely unmindful of the thudding in his jaw.

He approached the car warily. Its headlights were on, and the passenger compartment light was bright. A tractor-trailer rig blasted by, making the BMW sway and quiver.

Professor Willings put his hand on the glossy hood. The engine was off, choked out during the sudden deceleration. He raised himself on tiptoe and looked at the passenger compartment.

Empty.

He took a deep breath—a slow process through his clamped teeth—and walked over to the opened door. He got inside gingerly, like an old man. The radio was still on, playing a string interpretation of "The Girl From Ipanema." Professor Willings put his hands on the wheel and leaned his head against the padded hub, listening to his heartbeat slow down to normal.

Anxiety attack, he told himself. *Hospital drugs goofed me up, that's all.*

He sighed as he sat back up, reaching for the ignition.

There was a man in the headlight's beams, about a hundred feet away, walking toward the BMW.

The professor narrowed his eyebrows, puzzled. What on earth would someone be doing out here? Car trouble? Yet another hitchhiker? Whoever—it didn't look like someone with whom he wanted any nighttime dealings. Professor Willings twisted the key and the starter motor whinnied.

But the damned engine refused to catch.

Professor Willings cursed. He pressed the accelerator down and held it, then tried again. He watched the man as the starter turned over.

What does he want? Lift to a gas station? Money? God, why do these things have to happen to me?

Still, the engine would not catch. The man was sixty feet away.

Professor Willings stomped the accelerator three times, giving it more gas. It was strange, but the man's jacket looked a lot like that of the broad-shouldered fellow who'd been hitchhiking back at the hospital's entrance . . . which was impossible, of course. How could he have gotten here? Just some—God, who knew?

He turned the key again. The starter whinnied. *Come on, damn you!*

It turned over once, then died. There was a strong smell of gasoline.

Flooded! Professor Willings was about to bang his hand against the wheel, but froze. He stared ahead blankly.

The stranger had broken into a *run*. Was actually *grinning* as he came up on the headlights. Professor Willings felt the skin on his back start to shift and bunch. He grabbed the key and twisted it hard, holding it to the stops. The starter motor cranked on and on, and Professor Willings cried with equal parts of terror and frustration.

The man broke into a flat-out sprint, arms and legs raised high.

Professor Willings pushed the lock down, then leaned over to snap the lock on the passenger door. His heart beat like a trip-hammer. He stared at the approaching man with the dumb terror of an animal caught in headlight beams. The man reached the driver's door and grabbed the handle, pulling and yanking with enough force to make the car sway on its shocks.

Professor Willings pressed himself against the far door, staring at the man with stunned disbelief. He wanted to scream, to yell something that would make the stranger go away, but all that would come out of his wired jaw was an unintelligible warbling. The man started kicking the door, his face contorted with demonic fury. Then he suddenly jumped up to the hood and scampered over to the other side. He grabbed the passenger door's handle as Professor Willings clawed his way to the other side.

The professor cowered near the wheel, staring at the frenzied man with absolutely no comprehension of who this was or what he wanted or why this was happening. The BMW seesawed on its shocks. And then Professor Willings recognized that same baleful look, remembering it from that same crazy moment when his office door had suddenly splintered wide . . .

Professor Willings began screaming, the sound coming out as a high-pitched, quavering whinny.

The man picked up a rock and smacked it against the passenger window, chipping it. He smacked it again, and the window starred. The man grimaced as he brought it down again, and the rock broke through and tumbled into the leather seat.

He reached through and pulled up the lock.

Professor Willings opened the driver's door and tumbled to the asphalt. He quickly pushed himself up and ran out into the night, fleet on the wings of adrenaline. He ran away from the highway and into the knee-high sage, sure that if he could make it to the top of the hill he would be somehow safe. Blood pounded against his ears like twin pile drivers, and his chest had gone as cold as a deep freeze. The hill inclined steeply, and he started scrambling on all fours, pulling at the roots of dried bushes, grabbing at rocks that loosened and rolled downhill.

The hand clapped down on his neck like a blow, and his face slammed into the dirt. He felt the other hand grab on to his belt, and Professor Willings found himself lifted, brought back up to his feet, roughly turned around and forced back downhill, taking it in long, wide, looping steps that were only partly under his control.

Professor Willings tried to make his jaw open, the pain of the loosening wires totally unnoticed, sure that if he could only speak he could save himself, fall to his knees and beg for mercy, clapping his hands together and pleading and pleading and pleading. . . .

But things were happening much too rapidly now, much too fast for the professor to make any sense of it. They were almost upon the shiny gray BMW, muted "Ipanema" strains still coming from the radio. Professor Willings tried to turn around, but the man's grip was as strong as iron. They went by the car's trunk—the professor half-carried and half-skittering—and suddenly the man stopped, holding the professor near the edge of the highway.

A square-nosed tractor-trailer rig was coming down the near lane, and Professor Willings felt the hands on his neck and back tighten, getting him ready, the pavement humming and vibrating with growing intensity. . . .

His pants went damp with a gush of warm urine.

The wires in his jaw finally parted, and the scream burst into the night. The rig began blowing its horn in one continuous note, the sound becoming higher and higher in the doppler up-shift, and Professor Willings was shoved headlong into the night.

□

S E V E N

"Kathryn, this is the best food I've had in months."

She was surprised to feel a small rush of pleasure. "They're just cheeseburgers."

"What do you mean *just?*"

Marvin took another hefty bite, causing a ketchup-drenched pickle to slip out from under the bun. He chewed manfully, beaming with good cheer, the oversized burger firmly gripped between two hands.

Kathryn was glad she'd asked him in. It was fun having

someone in the house for a change. Or at least someone who wasn't peeled down to their designer shorts before the door closed. Cozy, too, even though the lack of a dining table forced them to sit cross-legged on the floor and use the coffee table.

Marvin swallowed audibly. "You know, you just don't seem like the type to make food like this."

"Oh? And what, pray, is my type food?"

"Well, like sprouts and stuff . . ." His face started to go pink. "I mean, you're in really good shape."

"I should be. I give workout classes four days a week. And as for burgers . . ." She had another bite and took her time chewing it. "I'm catching up. I was into sprouts *way* too long."

"Workout classes?"

"Yes, up in Hillcrest, at Windsong Aerobics. That and being manager here keep me fit."

"Sounds nice."

"It is. Lots of free time, really."

"You must need it to go through all these books.'

"What? Oh." The landscape of her apartment had become so familiar she barely noticed it anymore . . . and the guests she'd had of late hadn't been the sort to remark on the decor. Books were indeed a highlight, stacked everywhere there was a horizontal surface, even in small piles atop the stereo speakers.

"The collection of a perennial graduate student." Her smile was mocking. "Somehow I managed to keep everything from my college career."

"Which college was that?"

"Oh, gosh. Sometimes I think it'd be easier to list the colleges I *didn't* go to. But my only degree is from Berkeley, where I did my undergraduate work."

"Berkeley, wow. I'm impressed. That's a really good school."

"Yeah, it was supposed to be, but . . . academics weren't the big thing back then.'

"How so?"

There were three or four bites left to Kathryn's hamburger, but she was full. "Oh, you know. The great old days of Free Speech and Be-Ins and all that happy horseshit."

"Oh, yeah." Marvin smiled pleasantly. "The big Vietnam riots. Hippies and stuff. You were really into all that?"

Kathryn smiled and pushed her plate Marvin's way. "Want the rest?"

"You bet."

"It all seems so quaint now." Kathryn poured herself another glass of wine. "Like when you see those old silent movies from the turn of the century, with everyone walking around all rickety-tickety, like they weren't, you know, real people."

Marvin nodded, mouth full.

"But it was real, all right," Kathryn continued. "Real enough and big enough to eat you right up, if you weren't careful." She took a swallow of the wine.

Marvin paused in mid-bite. "How do you mean?"

Kathryn was looking at her wineglass, grinning a strange sort of half-grin. "It just sort of took over everything," she said quietly. "How you thought, how you dressed, what you wanted out of life . . . all of that was changed, turned around. I was so far into it I even . . . once I helped a man commit suicide."

Marvin stared. Kathryn looked up, giving him what she thought was a beautiful smile. But she looked as cold and eerie as a department store mannequin.

93

"What do you mean, 'helped'?"

"Just that. He wanted to do it, and I . . ." She had the wineglass by the stem, making the liquid swirl slowly. "He was a fellow who called himself Kartismanta, although his real name was Darryl Yates. He was a poet. A Post Minimalist."

"Post what?"

Kathryn ignored the question. She was looking at the wineglass, but her eyes had taken on a distant focus. The Kartismanta memory was out now, and she could see his sad, sweet face in the swirling wine, right down to the big droopy mustache and little wire-rimmed glasses.

"We met at a town called Vina," Kathryn said quietly. "A little place in the woods, ninety miles north of Sacramento. It was the site of an experimental writer's and artist's colony. He was sort of in charge of the Post Minimalist workshop, and that was what I was very much into back then." Her smile was lopsided, rueful. "He really liked my work."

She told him that two months into their affair Kartismanta opened the mailbox and found that his great work, *On the Mystery of My Being*, had been rejected by yet another literary journal, and he had looked at Kathryn with eyes that were sadder and sweeter than usual and announced that it was impossible to be truly sensitive and yet go on living in such a world.

"I thought that was heavy, you know? I didn't think regular people had it together enough to be sensitive like Kartismanta. Or me, even. Maybe me especially. You see, I was so sensitive I'd gotten a tubal ligation a couple of years before, in order to prevent bringing another life into such a venal bomb-threatened world." Kathryn grinned, but it was a strange sort of grin, full of aggression and derision.

"So I was right up there with Kartismanta. I could understand his sensitivity. Oh, never mind the fact that he turned forty on the very day he received that rejection. Never mind the fact that he'd been denied tenure at three different universities. Never mind the fact that he'd never been published on anything other than a mimeograph machine. He was above all that."

She told him how Kartismanta's last night was one of gentle ceremony. They read their favorite poems to each other, then made love by the light of a single flickering flame. They put on their jackets and went out into the wintry night, smiling bravely as fresh snow crunched under their boots. They came to a narrow bridge and Kartismanta sat on the rail and told Kathryn that he loved her, loved nature, loved all living things, and his spirit would soon be at peace. He sat there a long time, staring into space, his breath exhaling in great vaporous clouds. Kathryn was overcome by the poignancy of the moment, and Kartismanta told her not to weep, that even death was a beautiful thing. All he wanted was one last kiss.

"But when he reached out . . . it was only a narrow little railing, you see, and . . ."

She let the words trail off, unable to describe exactly how Kartismanta's eyes had gone wide with shock and terror behind the granny glasses as he lost his balance, how he grabbed desperately at air, and mostly, how terrible the sound was of him hitting the water, cutting through Kathryn's trance like a stick of dynamite.

"I rushed to the railing and looked over the side. God, I'd never seen anything look so black and cold as that river. There were even little ice floes. Kartismanta was hanging onto one, or at least trying to get a good grip on it, but it was just too small and slippery. His hair was all slicked down over his eyes, and I could even see glasses hanging on to one of his ears. And he was yelling. Dear Jesus, that *yelling . . .*"

The current was swift, and it quickly carried him under the bridge. She rushed to the other side and caught a glimpse of him thrashing away into the darkness, screaming her name over and over.

"I ran down to the riverbank, and began stumbling through the ankle-deep snow, trying to follow him. I kept calling, but all I could hear was the rushing of the water. I must have stumbled through that snow for a mile before I decided to go back to town for help.

"It was two days before the search party found him, and . . . I just couldn't look at him when those grappling hooks broke surface.

"Things changed after that." Kathryn looked cool and serene, Marvin thought. A cold elegance, like an ancient marble bust. "The movement started to lose some of its benign psychedelic glow. And I began to suspect that I might as well have gotten my degree in Home Ec and gone on to the stewardess academy at Eastern Airlines, for all I'd learned about myself in the so-called 'Movement.' My God, look at the time."

She got up and took Marvin's plate. "I hope I haven't ruined your dinner."

"Oh, no. Really." He got up, following her into the kitchenette. "That was some . . . story. What did you do after that?"

"Nothing very interesting, I'm afraid." She scraped the hamburger remains into a plastic grocery bag hung underneath the sink. "I went back to L.A. to see my folks. One of my friends wrote and asked if I wanted to teach Hatha Yoga at the Universal Consciousness Center here. That, believe it or not, was the forerunner of Windsong Aerobics,

Incorporated." Kathryn put the plastic dishpan in the sink and began filling it with water. "Listen, I've got a really long day tomorrow."

"Well, uh . . ." He tried not to sound disappointed. "Thanks for the dinner, then."

She didn't turn from the dishes. "No problem."

He went to the door, wondering why she had become so distant when things had started off so well. He opened the door and turned to say good night, and saw that Kathryn was standing right behind him.

"Listen"—she was wearing a half-smile—"I really appreciate you're staying for dinner tonight. I'm sorry I . . . well, I didn't think it would turn into a one-sided conversation. I wanted to ask you all about your paintings."

Marvin beamed. "Sure, great. Anytime."

"Name it."

"Sometime . . . tomorrow?"

"Sure, tomorrow."

E I G H T

The nurse had picked up the untouched tray hours ago, murmuring something about how pitiful it was to see such a pretty girl turn to skin and bones, and how they were going to be forced to use an intravenous feed if she continued losing weight. Genevieve had paid her as much attention as she had her parents earlier in the day, who had pleaded and wept and begged until it became as tiresome as a rerun of "The Price Is Right" on the set bolted to the wall.

They couldn't help her. No one could. Especially when you weren't sure if you wanted to be helped at all. . . .

She rolled onto her side and stared at the window, watching the stars come out. *Star light, star bright . . .*

He made her feel so lost and tiny, as if she were a wanderer on a fleshy desert of enormous pectorals and ribbed abdominals. A carnal universe, swirling around a penis grown to the size of a whale—forever turgid and unsatisfied, banging, pummeling, jabbing, finally lifting her high as if impaling her on a spear, her limbs hanging limp and useless, her lungs no longer capable of taking a breath, eyes rolled back as she was paraded before a jungle tribe that howled with acclaim, banging their hollowed-out logs as they danced, making a din that overcame the deepness of the night. . . .

She closed her eyes and gripped the pillow so tightly it began to hurt her fist. He took her to terrible places, evil and vile and full of unwanted secrets, but oh God oh God how it made everything else seem pale and washed out and unreal—

He was there. She sensed it, and the breath in her lungs went cold. She turned from the window and saw him looming over her, a broad-shouldered, masculine silhouette, completely dark, utterly faceless.

He grabbed the blanket and flicked it from the bed in one swift motion. She lifted up her arms and he pulled the nightgown off, then the bed sagged as he climbed in and straddled her chest and she felt his strong hands wrap around her head like a vise and he brought her face up and started working her skull like a piston, grunting and sighing, and when he tired of that he laid back and drew her on top of him and held her upright with one hand and used the other to work her hips in precisely the way he wanted, and she began to gasp with exhaustion, feeling herself become as weak and inanimate as a straw doll, and just when she thought she knew how he wanted her to move she found herself pushed back on the bed and flipped around and drawn up so that his hands were tight on her rump and he pulled and pushed and bounced her off his crotch and she tried to keep herself up on all fours but it went on so long that exhaustion finally overcame her and she collapsed, arms and legs completely limp, but that made no difference to him, he only held her hips more firmly in place and worked all the more strenuously, making her head jog against the pillow, stinging her buttocks with the force of his hammering, and then he suddenly disengaged himself and twisted her into a new position, her arms and legs rolling limply, and it went on for hours without end, without break, without mercy.

N I N E

he restaurant was festooned with fishing nets whose cork floats had gone gray with age, and the swordfish on the far wall was covered with dust. But Kathryn thought the view of the Pacific more than made up for the overly fried food, and she looked at the sunset for so long that she started to see purple dots in front of her eyes.

"Is your food okay?" Marvin asked.

"It's just fine." She blinked and returned to her forgotten meal. "But you really didn't have to bring me here."

"Oh, hey, it's nothing. I mean, it's my pleasure." He looked so goofily anxious that Kathryn had to catch herself from smiling. "It's the least I could do, after last night."

"Really, I would've been just as happy with . . . this is fine, Marvin. You're sweet to have brought me here. Thank you."

He grinned with happy relief.

Kathryn's fork crunched through the flounder as if it were a potato chip. "Have you been painting long?"

"Since I can remember, I guess." He forked in a mouthful of something that might have been either scallops or hush puppies. "But I've only tried oils in the last couple of months. They're . . . difficult."

"I think you're very talented."

He blushed. "Thanks."

"No, I mean it. Did you study art in college?"

He'd been going through the deluxe seafood platter like a steamroller, but he suddenly paused. "No."

"But didn't you say something about going to UCSD?"

"Accounting was my major."

"Accounting? How did you get into that?"

"It's a long story."

"Well, I'd like to hear it, Marvin. If you don't mind."

He poured the remainder of his Dos Equis into the mug. He told the story of his brief collegiate sojourn, eyes never once meeting Kathryn's. But she watched him with interest. At times he seemed to be angry with himself, then his anger would abruptly shift to his father, and Kathryn watched how his face would change from something that was soft and boyish to a mask that looked like an artifact from a medieval dungeon.

"Wow. So he kicked you out. That's unbelievable. I can't imagine anyone being so shitty."

"I wasn't exactly what you would call his favorite."

Kathryn poured the last bit of wine from the carafe into her glass. "And you never talked with him again?"

"Not until about a year later, after I'd joined the Navy, when I got into some . . . trouble."

"You were in the Navy?"

He looked rueful. "Yeah. You see, I just couldn't handle working full-time and going to school. I'd always heard that the service had a lot of educational opportunities, and veterans' benefits are supposed to be . . ." He shrugged. "I bought it, anyway. Signed up."

The sun had dipped below the horizon, and stars were just beginning to dust the sky. "Tell me about it, Marvin. Really, I'm interested."

"Well, I went to boot camp right here in San Diego. It wasn't anything like I expected." He smiled. "They shaved me bald and put me in a barracks with forty other guys, all of us scared shitless. The typical day started off about four-thirty with these petty officers screaming at us and throwing garbage cans down the aisles between the racks, and it kind of went downhill from there. . . .

"I was too scared to do anything but follow orders. I didn't even have time to think about how this was the hardest thing I'd ever been through. At least, not until one morning when we found this guy in the shower with his wrists all slashed up."

"My God. You're kidding."

"Oh, no. Not at all. Some people just couldn't hack it."

"But . . . you did."

He looked surprised. "Yeah. I guess I did at that."

The waitress, a tough old bird who didn't approve of any lollygagging when people should be eating, asked if they were finished with their meal. Both plates were still half-full, but it'd been a while since either had touched anything. Marvin told her to take the plates away and ordered another

103

beer for himself. He asked if Kathryn wanted a refill on the carafe, but she shook her head.

"Things in the company changed after that," Marvin said. "We all started pulling together, helping each other out. And when the next batch of recruits came through, me and my buddies would laugh at how screwed up they were on the parade ground."

Kathryn grinned. "Your buddies, huh?"

"Yeah, my old buds." He smiled, shaking his head. "Strange group. I'd never met guys like that before, not in high school, not in UCSD. And not just because a lot of them came from poor families. They treated me a lot different than . . ."

He looked down at the beer bottle, searching for words while he peeled at the label with his thumbnail. "You see, a lot of people gave me a hard time in high school. And in college nobody really gives a shit about anything except partying and grades. But the guys in my company treated me different. They treated me . . . well, it was more than being *liked*. It was being, you know, respected."

"Because of your size?"

"Huh?"

"Well, you're pretty tall, Marvin. Pretty . . . broad across the shoulders." She swirled the wine in the glass. "In a group of men like that, I think it counts for a lot."

He smiled slowly. "Well, one guy didn't. Little fellow, too. He was an *angry* son of a bitch, always mad as hell about something. His name was Sal DiStefano, a kid from New Jersey.

"He started pushing me around one night, about six weeks into boot camp, just before lights out. Jabbed his finger in my chest and started saying stuff like 'Come on, big guy, you don't look so tough to me.'

"It made me feel sick to my stomach. I just kept backing

104

up and he kept pushing and I tripped over this rack and fell over backward.

"The guys started laughing like hell. Like this time in high school, when I was at a football tryout. . . ." Marvin grimaced. "I don't know what happened, but something went off inside my head like a hand grenade, and I was off the deck and on top of that wop before he knew what was going on, just pounding the living fuck out of—oh, excuse me."

Kathryn almost asked him what the problem was, then smiled. "Quite all right. Go on."

"Anyway, next day me and Sal are at this thing called Captain's Mast. The guy in charge was this old commander with about a million ribbons, and Christ did he ever chew our asses out. Ended up fining us a hundred bucks each, gave us extra duty for the rest of boot camp, and restricted us to the base.

"But that was it. I couldn't believe how relieved I was. And that night, when everyone was getting ready to climb into the rack, Sal came up to me and shook my hand, then announced to the barracks that we were buddies."

Marvin shook his head, smiling. "The rest of boot camp went fast. In fact, we almost made Honor Company. We all went out on the town after graduation, and everyone was really kind of sad to see the gang breaking up. But we were all anxious to get on with our orders, too.

"Mine were for radioman 'A' school, right at the same base, if you can believe it. It was a lot better deal than boot camp. The barracks were more like dorms, and there was liberty most every night. The school itself was a bitch though, really a lot harder than anything I'd taken in college. But I was eating it up. You see, after 'A' school I was supposed to go to submarine school, then go out to the fleet in a boomer, one of those huge ballistic missile boats."

Marvin looked out the big picture window. A commercial fishing boat was running close inshore, big floodlights trained on its wake. "It's hard to describe how I felt. I'd seen movies like *Run Silent Run Deep* ever since I was a little kid, and it just seemed . . . incredible that I could be a part of something like that. A crew member of a submarine."

Kathryn was fascinated by the look on his face, by its sweet poignancy. But the sweetness quickly faded and lines bracketed his mouth. "I was halfway through 'A' school when it happened. Sal gave me a call. He was finishing up boiler technician 'A' school and already had orders to a frigate. He and some of his BT friends were having a little graduation party. Plus it was the start of the Thanksgiving holiday, a four-day weekend. Hell, I didn't have anywhere else to go.

"The party was at this crummy motel a few blocks from the base, and when I got there Sal and his buddies were already working on their second quart of Wild Turkey. There was a huge ghetto blaster on the bureau and it was tuned way up on something like Ratt or Twisted Sister, something with a lot of angry screaming and yelling.

"They were a tough-looking bunch. A couple of them already had tattoos. But they accepted me right away, just like that. It was stupid of me, but . . . I was kind of flattered, in a way. I started drinking pretty heavily. And one of them had some dope.

"Things got dizzy as the night wore on. The phone rang once, and Sal said it was the manager, asking us to keep it down. We all had a good laugh over that. Two of the BTs went out for a supply run around eleven or so, and when they came back they had this woman with them. She was a, you know . . ."

He looked down at the plastic tablecloth, and even in the subdued lighting Kathryn could see his face reddening. "God, was she ever ugly. And *mean*—Jesus! She wanted . . . a certain amount of money from each guy, but Sal negotiated it way down. Then she stripped down to her undies and joined in on the party, dancing and everything. After a few pulls off that Wild Turkey she started to loosen up and not act so mean and sour, and along about one o'clock she started, well, doing her job."

Marvin sat back in the chair. "I'd never been so drunk in my life. I found myself flat on my back, laughing like hell while a couple of the guys were pulling off my pants for my turn." He smiled thinly. "That was when the door busted open. Two big cops barged in with their nightsticks drawn and told us to freeze. There were another two cops outside arresting the guys who tried to jump out the bathroom window. It's all really hazy now, but I kind of remember the inside of this police cruiser, then I was turned over to the Shore Patrol, and they threw me in the brig."

He leaned forward, looking tired. "This time there wasn't any Captain's Mast, not for what I'd done. I was scheduled for a full-blown court-martial. They assigned this JAG lieutenant as my defense counsel. He said the thing with the drugs was the worst—the Navy was really coming down hard on drugs, kicking people out right and left—but at least when it came to something like marijuana, enlisted men were given a second chance. *Usually*, that is. He said this thing about fighting in boot camp wasn't going to help any. And of course there was the stuff about soliciting for prostitution and being drunk and disorderly and resisting arrest. He kept shaking his head and saying that things looked pretty bad.

"I really needed some help, so I . . . called home. I just didn't know what else to do. Christ, was my father ever angry. It'd been a year since I talked to him, and he said I had treated them really shabby, not letting them know whether I was alive or dead, Mom worried sick, on and on. And that was *before* I told him about the trouble I was in. But when I did . . . when I did . . ."

He squeezed his eyes tight and ran his hand across his face, and Kathryn thought he was going to break down. But Marvin quickly regained his composure, straightened up, and neatly clasped his hands on the table as if presenting himself for a job interview.

"He just laughed," he said quietly. "That same laugh he used when he kicked me out. He told me he hoped my mother never found out what a fuckup I'd become, because it would just break her heart. He started yelling about a lot of other stuff, but I just put the receiver back down. I . . . haven't talked with him since."

Marvin stared at his hands, feeling so terrible he wished he hadn't told his story after all. What good had it done? And what must Kathryn think of him now? All he wanted was for her to think well of him, and now he had shown—

Then her hand was on his.

Marvin lay awake long into the night, hands clasped behind his head, staring at the ceiling. He wondered if he had done the right thing, just telling her good night like that. He wondered if he should have tried to kiss her, or what might have happened had he had courage enough to ask himself in for a drink.

God, what he'd give to be in her apartment right now. And not just because of the sex. How he longed to be drifting into sleep with someone beside him, a friend, a companion. . . .

Ah, but is that really the truth?

The voice came up smoothly, effortlessly.

Isn't there something more that you want besides a warm body laying next to yours? Like maybe having your pole inside that warmth, pummeling and driving away, going

without end at the sweetest little chore in the world? Aren't you just dying to know what it's like?

Marvin grimaced. Maybe he should go down to the Handy Andy for a six-pack, but . . . the sleepy feeling suddenly came to his eyes, as if it had been turned on with a switch. He rolled onto his side and began to feel dreamy and weightless, and images of Kathryn and Genevieve and his parents paraded by, and then the big revolving Sup'r Serv sign floated up, sagging telephone lines and palm trees in the background.

And as he tottered on the edge of unconsciousness he felt that effortless little tug, making him finally spiral down into the black void like an airplane out of control, and at the bottom there was a building by itself on a grassy hill, and he knew there was a room in there somewhere where a scarecrow-thin girl was sitting up in her darkened room, pulling the night-gown off over her head. . . .

□

T E N

Marvin took a likely-looking socket from the tray and fitted it onto the air-powered drill. He tested the trigger lightly as he stepped over to the pickup. The socket's fit was snug—*Hey, whadd'ya know? Guessed right the first time*—and he spun the bolts off in short order, whistling under his breath.

Tire rotation was a simple job, but he could use one hand to count the number of times he'd been allowed to work in the service bay. It was a lot more interesting than running the pumps, not to mention more lucrative if you could get slotted in as a mechanic.

Marvin was about to tackle the last tire, the left front, when the service bell dinged. He put the drill back on the workbench, making sure the slack part of the air line trollied back up into the receiver, and went out to an old but nicely maintained Ford Fairlane, bright blue. He wore his best smile as he went up to the driver's window.

The gray-haired lady said she wanted premium, and Marvin set the pump on automatic and started cleaning the windows. It was another fine day all right, and he'd even caught himself carrying a tune during his morning shower.

He wondered if being happy on the inside made a difference to those around you. Mr. Sam acted kind of surprised when he made a sour comment about Marvin's Datsun and Marvin turned it into a joke and tossed it right back at him. And later on, when he was just minding his own business and running the pumps, Mr. Sam had come up and told him about the job on the pickup and to handle it whenever the fill-up action was slow.

"I don't know what's different about you, Moy," he'd said, "but I got to admit you look like you can handle a little more action than the pumps."

Mr. Sam had been pleased, somehow. At least in his way. And Marvin was surprised at the satisfaction it gave him.

He made change for the lady and thanked her, then went walking back to the service bay lightly. Dell and J.J. were at work on a little MGB over at the far bay, their hands greasy, conferring with each other like a pair of surgeons getting ready for a triple bypass.

Marvin got the last tire off the pickup and set it aside. He started looking for the laminated tire-rotation checksheet, but it wasn't anywhere to be found. He walked over to the MGB, getting ready to ask the pair if they'd seen it recently. Not that he really *had* to—it was just that he wanted to talk to them mechanic-to-mechanic like, instead of like a know-nothing gas jockey to the Lords Almighty.

They were talking quietly but shut up as soon as Marvin came within earshot.

"Excuse me, guys, but have you seen—"

Dell's face was blank and impassive. "Fuck off."

Marvin stopped, feeling his face redden. He turned around and walked away. He thought for sure they were going to start laughing, but they remained strangely quiet. He rummaged for the checksheet by the parts books and found it wedged up near the grease-stained Yellow Pages.

When he got back to his apartment he found a big folder lying up against his door. It was huge—better than a yard on each side—with little plastic carrying handles. He'd seen things like this at the UCSD bookstore, stock items for the fine arts students. Portfolios.

Marvin took it inside and opened it. There was a yellow Post-it note stuck to the inside: *Thought you might need this. K.*

He smiled. A present. An honest-to-goodness present. The first one anyone had given him in a long, long time.

He decided to go over to Kathryn's apartment, and a little part of him was mildly surprised that he did it without any hint of bashfulness. He went upstairs just as bold as you please and knocked on the door. A shadow passed over the peephole, and then the door swung open.

"Hi." She had a towel over her shoulder and there were tiny soapsuds near her hairline.

"Hello. I came by to say thanks for the present."

"Thought you might. Come on in."

Kathryn shut the door and went to the bathroom. "I was

just getting ready for my evening session at Windsong."
She splashed water on her face, rinsing away the last bit of
soap, then began drying her face. "They asked me if I
wouldn't mind taking Tuesdays as well, and I said sure, I
need the money."

Marvin grinned. "It's not as if you need the exercise. You
look great."

"Well, thank *you*." She came into the living room wearing
electric-blue leotards with a pink bikini-type bottom and
looking great indeed. She started putting things in a designer gym bag.

"What made you buy the portfolio?"

"Oh, I just *happened* to have a chat with one of the ladies
in my class who *happens* to own a gallery downtown." She
looked up and grinned. "Since you've got an appointment
with her Friday, I thought you'd need something nice to
carry your work."

"*Huh?*"

She zipped up the bag. "You heard me, big fella. Gallery
Works. Five P.M., Friday. Don't be late, and make sure it's
your best stuff."

Marvin watched blankly as Kathryn pulled on an oversized gray sweatshirt. "Gosh, Kathryn, I . . ."

She took his arm and began ushering him outside. "Come
on, I'm gonna be late."

"But I'm not ready to—"

"*Sure* you are. Your stuff is great." She pulled the door
shut and made sure it was locked. "Mary will flip when
she sees that self-portrait. I told her all about it. Make sure
you bring that especially."

They walked downstairs and out to the front of the building, where Kathryn kept her aging Volvo at the curb.

"I just don't know if I can get ready in time."

"Then you have a lot to do before Friday, don't you?"

113

He gestured helplessly, smiling lopsidedly. "How can I thank you?"

"Didn't I tell you?" She grabbed his elbow, got up on tiptoe, and gave him a quick kiss on the lips. "I'm your agent, baby. We're in this together. I'm gonna get rich off my ten percent. See you later."

Marvin watched her drive off, wondering which had startled him more. The news about the gallery . . . or the sudden kiss.

He spent a long time going through his drawings, sorting out piles of things that were ready to show, things that needed a little more work, and stuff that was entirely useless.

He finally had them arranged by nine o'clock, and was almost ready to start on the more-work pile. Almost ready, save for his rumbling hunger. He put on a sweatshirt and locked up, then jogged down to the business district for a quick sandwich and a beer.

He ate at a brightly lit deli facing the ocean. There were bonfires dotting the beach, and he felt a warm tingle of satisfaction when he realized he envied the revelers not at all. There was so much waiting for him back at the Cota Arms. . . .

When he returned he bounded up the stairs, and when he reached the small balcony he paused to look at Kathryn's bedroom window. She was back from her exercise class. There was only a dim light in her window, perhaps from the opened door of the bathroom.

Marvin wondered what it would be like to be lying in her bed, impatient for the bathroom light to flick out. And how his lungs would go breathlessly cold as she padded across the room, her nakedness defined by the pale moonlight. And it would be so easy just to . . . just to drift over there, take a little look . . .

Marvin gripped the balcony railing hard. *No, don't even think about it. It wouldn't be right, not when things have started off so—*

He began to feel ill. Dizzy. *It couldn't be happening, could it? Not now; not so easily. No!*

But when he looked at her window he saw that things had already begun to change, with faint, underexposed images shifting across her bedroom window in a slow, nonsensical montage.

No! Don't! Stop it!

He turned to his door and opened it wide, grimly determined to proceed with the evening as planned, to get on with the business of working on his drawings, to just ignore—

It was black as pitch in the room. He couldn't find the light switch; he couldn't find *anything*. But he went farther into the darkness, feeling his way by running his hand across the wall, dreadfully sure that if he went back outside he would be stepping into Kathryn's bedroom, and that would be—

Aw come on, Marv, we're talking prime beef over there, I mean *prime*; 'course old Genevieve's still got a few good bounces left in her, maybe we could go over there first—

—wrong, so horribly wrong, so the thing was to keep moving, keep looking for the light switch; everything would be okay as soon as he found the light switch. He felt his way toward the bathroom, and the wallpaper's smooth texture gave way to something that was as coarse and brittle as brick, and he snatched his hand away. He had never been in darkness so complete and he looked around for any

115

sign of light, even back to the opened door of his room, but there was nothing now, he might as well have been inside an unlighted bank vault, and just as panic began to creep in he finally discerned a light, distant and murky and unreal, and he moved toward it warily, the images around him slowly taking shape, and a silhouette flitted by—

Last call, jerkface, last call; Genevieve's the *other* way—

—until he recognized it as an alleyway of some sort, brick walls to either side, and then he was out of it and on the split concrete of an old sidewalk.

He recognized the location at once. Hattstaedt's Sup'r Serv was just across the street, lights off and closed up. It was very late, with some fog rolling in and no traffic in sight.

There was a distant metallic clang, like the sound of a steel tool dropped on concrete. Marvin looked up and saw something that hadn't been apparent before, something that wasn't right about Hattstaedt's Sup'r Serv. A glossy Chevy van was backed up against one of the service bays. Which was *open*, by God. . . .

And then he was suddenly before the station office, lights off, but with the door wide open. He looked inside and sucked in his breath when he saw Mr. Sam. . . .

He was on his back, lying by the map rack, tied up and unconscious. Or maybe even dead. A thin trail of blood seeped from the back of his head. There was some kind of gag in his mouth, an oily sponge secured with several turns of duct tape.

Marvin went inside, but before he could get on his knees to assist Mr. Sam, his attention was drawn to the door that led to the service bays. It was open, and Marvin could see the men on the other side of it, even though they were shadowy and indistinct in the weak glow of a battery-powered lantern.

There was a sudden clang as another tool dropped to the floor, and Marvin heard J.J.'s muted cursing. Then he recognized the voice of Dell Ready, telling J.J. to keep it down. Another man, a stranger, passed by silently, a Michelin Steel Radial slung underneath each arm. He tossed them in the back of the van, then headed back toward the tire rack, which, Marvin saw, was just about empty.

He noted that all the big tool boxes were gone, as were the better pieces of test equipment. Air hoses were dangling from the overhead racks, their power tools detached. Marvin looked through the office window and saw that the cash register was empty, save for a loose scattering of checks and credit card slips . . . and then Marvin was doing nothing more than staring at the dark outlines of the furniture in his own room, staring at them with as much wonder as he had viewed the scene at Hattstaedt's. . . .

He shook his head roughly, squeezing his eyes tight. When he opened them again he saw that he was still in his room, the desk and bed half-lit from the opened door to the balcony.

He walked out onto the balcony and breathed deeply of the cool, moist air. The fog was coming in thicker now, a little bit heavier than he'd seen over at—

It's still going on, numbnuts! Call the police before it's too late!

He went downstairs quickly, feeling in his pocket for the keys to his Datsun, but couldn't find them. He turned around and started heading back up, then thought about how long it would take to drive the four blocks to the public phone at the U-Tote-'Em.

But Kathryn's light was still on . . .

He ran back down the steps, across the back yard, and

opened the back door to the main house. He went down the narrow hallway, up the staircase, then began banging on the old mahogany door so hard it rattled in its frame.

"*Who is it? Who's out there?*" There was a shrill edge to her voice. Only then did Marvin realize that what he was doing might strike her as completely mad.

"Kathryn, it's me," he said in a loud whisper. "I need to use your phone, it's an emergency. I've got to call the police."

The little peephole darkened for a moment, then the door was opened only as far as the chain would allow. She had on reading glasses that were shaped like little half-moons. "What did you say?"

"The gas station I work at is being robbed!"

"What? When?"

"Now! It's happening now!"

"Wha—how do you know?"

"*I just do!*" He immediately lowered his voice. "I mean, well, it's just something I *know*. Please believe me."

She had looked frightened at first, but her expression had changed to one of bafflement.

Marvin had an inspiration. "Look, why don't you call the police yourself? For me? I'll give you the address."

She took off the reading glasses and looked at him oddly. "I . . . I think that'd be best, Marvin. Under, you know, the circumstances. . . ."

"Fine! Fine! It's Hattstaedt's Sup'r Serv, down at the corner of Mason and Voltaire. Got it?"

"Yes. You stay right here."

The door clunked closed and there was the metallic snick of the automatic lock. Marvin ran his hand across his forehead, wiping away sweat that wasn't there. His mind boiled with an uneven mixture of confusion and consternation, and he didn't know whether to be more upset about the robbery or the lunatic impression he was making on Kathryn. He balled his fist and pounded it against his knee. Stupid! *Stupid!*

The door opened, again only as far as the chain would allow. "Marv?"

"Yes?"

"They said they'll check it out right away."

"Thanks, Kathryn." He started to go, but stopped. "Listen, I'm really sorry to have . . . disturbed you like this."

"Oh, no, really." The door was still firmly chained.

"Well, if it wasn't something important, believe me, I wouldn't . . ." He looked at her helplessly. "Good night, anyway, Kathryn. I've got to get going."

"Where? To that place?"

"Yeah. I'm sure the police would want . . . well, I just think I should go over there."

Marvin looked at the face behind the door. For a moment he let himself believe that the door would fly open and, like some willful heroine in an old movie, she would come rushing out, saying that there was no stopping her, she was going with him, dammit.

But the face behind the door was wary, and Marvin let the fantasy wisp into nothing.

"Good night, Kathryn. Thanks again."

She didn't say anything as he pounded downstairs, heading back to his apartment to find the Datsun's keys.

□

E L E V E N

Marvin drove as fast as he dared, but when he was half a block from the gas station he turned off the engine and coasted the rest of the way, lights off. His excitement changed to sickening nausea when he saw there was absolutely no sign of life at Hattstaedt's Sup'r Serv.

He eased the Datsun to the curb opposite the gas station, set the parking brake, and got out. He started walking toward the station, wondering if his vision had been true after all. What if a dozen squad cars suddenly showed up, only to find nothing? Wasn't there a harsh penalty for phoning in a false report? Then, with an ice-cold bolt of adrenaline, he saw the van in the shadows by the service bays. A big Econoline, just like . . .

He stepped onto the station's curb, his eyes and ears cocked to extreme readiness. There was some movement at the rear of the van, and then he heard soft cursing, quickly suppressed.

It is going on! It's really happening! He stepped behind the phone booth at the far corner of the station and peered around the side. The van trembled slightly as one last item was loaded aboard, then there was a quick double-*thunk* as its doors slammed closed. Marvin wondered if he should slip in the booth and try calling the police again. Maybe Kathryn hadn't even really called! He was feeling in his pocket for change when the service bay door came racketing down with a bang.

Then, on the far side of the gas station, he noticed a growing luminescence of flashing red and blue. No siren was used, and the patrol car suddenly careened into view. There was a loud squeal of brakes as it came to a halt.

The three burglars acted instantly. They broke and ran in the direction opposite from the cruiser.

Another police car screamed into view on the other side of the station, blocking their exit. The men swerved and began running toward the phone booth, legs pumping, jackets fluttering behind them. Marvin backed away from the booth, shocked, not knowing what to do.

Another cruiser came onto the scene, roaring down the same street Marvin had used. It stopped right next to him, and he was stunned by the red-and-blue explosions of its light bar. Suddenly Marvin found himself slammed up

121

against the phone booth, a huge cop pressing his thick forearm against Marvin's throat and holding a service revolver to his face.

Things happened fast. Marvin heard the shouts of the police as they closed in on the trio. There was a grunt and the sounds of a scuffle. Out of the corner of his eye Marvin saw J.J. caught by a flying tackle. Then Marvin felt himself being lifted and he skittered along on tiptoe as the cop shoved him toward the patrol car. He was slammed across the hood and felt himself being frisked. Then his arms were yanked behind him and he felt the coldness of a handcuff slapped across his wrist.

"Wait! *Wait!*" It was a woman's voice, and Marvin craned his neck up and saw that it was Kathryn, running from across the street. Her parked Volvo was in the background, the driver's door open. Relief and gratitude flooded over him in a wave. "Wait, officer! That man's with me! We're the ones who called it in."

The cop was dubious at first, but he listened to Kathryn's story. Finally, he let Marvin up, but he held on to his arm until a sergeant came up, listened to Kathryn, and ordered Marvin let go.

"Sorry, fella." The cop had a shy little grin for such a big guy. "You know how it goes sometimes."

Marvin massaged his wrist and was about to say something to the officer, but his eyes were drawn to Dell Ready, not more than ten yards away. He was on his knees, arms clamped behind him by two cops. They hauled him to his feet roughly, and Dell saw Marvin by the cruiser.

"*You!*" Dell stared at him in astonishment, then with dreadful comprehension. "*You* were the one who called the cops, you goddamn shitstick!"

The cops began dragging him away. Marvin saw J.J. and

the other guy being shoved into the rear of another cruiser. Dell looked at Marvin over his shoulder, glaring at him with nightmarish intensity.

"I'll get you for this, Marvin! I swear to Christ I'll get you! You hear me! *I'll get your fucking ass for this!*"

□

T W E L V E

Sergeant Perry thought, Poor stupid slob.

The coffee shop was three blocks from the police station, handy for private conversations. Marvin sat on the opposite side of the booth, totally absorbed in the task of stirring coffee that had no cream or sugar. There was a big picture window just behind him, old and hazed around the edges, and it gave onto a view of the harbor that was Chamber-of-Commerce perfect. The sky was achingly blue, the temperature exactly right, and a big white passenger liner was slowly working its way into the harbor, trying to avoid a flotilla of lazily tacking sailboats.

The detective had long ago learned that the most important lesson of police work was not to get personally involved. Kind of a Catch-22, since the typical cop *was* the sort of person who wanted to get involved. And brother, he should know. His stint on Homicide had cost him dear. Couldn't hack that shit at *all* . . . at least, not when it came down to the cases involving children.

Still, he'd learned to maintain a certain detachment from the people his work brought him in contact with, although it wasn't foolproof. As was the case here now. How could he not feel sorry for this Moy kid? Saves a business from getting ripped off, maybe even his boss' life, and what does he get for his trouble?

A big, fat shoeprint on the ass.

Perry had first heard about it the day before yesterday, shortly after the Hattstaedt robbery had gone down. He was intrigued by the fact that Marvin's name had come up once again, and he sought out a detailed briefing from the investigating officers. It seemed like the standard citizen-hero story . . . except for the twist about Moy getting fired. That was the incredible part. Enough so that Perry eventually found himself at the gas station, looking for Mr. Sam.

The skinny old redneck had been working the pumps, a Budweiser baseball cap covering most of the bandage on his head.

"Yeah, I gave that fuckpoke the boot. So what?"

"But he was the one who—"

"Oh, yeah man! Sure! He was just as sweet 'n' pure as Little Bo Peep!" He returned the nozzle to the pump and slapped the cutoff lever. Then he gave Perry a stupid-sly grin. "He weren't the one that called it in, right? He was right here, wasn't he? Right here with the rest of them thieves."

"The woman who called it in said—"

Mr. Sam cackled. "She stuck up for him because she's his *girlfriend*, you goddamn idiot! What do you expect?" He turned his head and spat, then wiped his mouth with the back of his hand. "Just because *you* buy that story don't mean *I* have to. And it sure the fuck don't mean I don't have the right to throw whoever the hell I want of'n my property."

"You son of a bitch." Perry clenched his fists tightly. "That kid saved you from being cleaned out. And if the paramedics hadn't come when they did you wouldn't be here pumping gas right now, you know that? Huh? You realize you may owe him your *life*?"

Mr. Sam's eyes got tiny and hard, just like the eyes of the monstrous hogs Perry had seen on his uncle's farm, years ago. "Then make me take him back, Mr. Officer! Show me the law that says I can't fire whoever the fuck I want! Show me!"

Perry turned his back and walked away, fists still tightly clenched. He was so mad he was afraid he might've punched out the old coot's headlamps, given another second. He got into his car and slammed the door, and was surprised to see that Mr. Sam had followed him.

"You tell that shitbird if I see him again he's a dead man!" Mr. Sam shook his gnarled fist. "Bought me a fucking Magnum, and if I see his sorry ass again I'll blow his brains out all over this asphalt! You tell him that, you hear? Tell him, Sergeant!"

Perry blew on his coffee before taking a sip. Marvin had stopped stirring but continued to stare into nothingness.

The thing with Marvin's boss was bad enough, Perry

thought, but what really took the cake was that Dell Ready character. Perry had sat in on one of Ready's interrogations and the guy was classic hard case. Kept the lid on pretty good, too; cool as a refrigerated cucumber. Except when it came to the subject of Marvin Moy. Then he'd loose control a little bit—grimacing, clenching his hands into tight balls, letting some heat creep into his voice. But even though it was clear he intended to make it his business to get on Marvin's case, he was smart enough not to make any overt threats, and he even disavowed the one he'd made during the arrest. When he finally posted bail, there was nothing they could do.

Marvin had, in fact, come to the police station only this morning to check on Ready's status. Perry had seen him at the front desk and walked over. Told him that Ready had thrown bail. Marvin took it kind of hard, and Perry had decided to ask him out for a cup of coffee, for a little talk. Marvin's smile was shy and hesitant.

Perry drained the last drops from his cup. He wondered what he could possibly say to the boy. *Tough toots, kid, but that's the way she goes. Find another job, and keep a sharp lookout for good old Dell.* He watched the plump waitress pour a fresh cup of coffee. Her ample bosom blocked out the view of the harbor, and when she was gone he saw that the passenger liner was making its approach on the B Street pier—right across the street—a tugboat snugged up against her bow.

"So tell me, Marvin. How's the job hunt going?"

"Not so good. I checked out the warehouses over by the Gaslamp Quarter this morning. Nothing available right now." He sighed. "They said try again next week."

Perry nodded. He knew it must be rough. The service station operators had their own little grapevine, and the word on Marvin wouldn't be good. And Perry knew about

Marvin's less-than-honorable, too—a copy of his discharge papers was in the Collier/Willings file. Correction—the *Collier* file. The good professor was now the late professor, having met with some kind of grotesque accident after leaving the hospital. The report indicated he'd been run down on I-5 late at night after his car had broken down.

"Well, listen," Perry said, "you need a reference, give them my name. Okay?"

"Sure, thanks." Marvin started to get out of the booth.

"And also . . ." Perry opened his wallet and slid a card across the formica. "Call me if Ready starts bothering you. We know exactly how to take care of that kind of trouble, and fast."

Marvin took it. "Thank you."

They went outside. The passenger liner was tied up now, and a stream of tourists was filing down a bright blue gangway.

"Can I give you a lift, Marvin?"

"No thanks, Sergeant. I want to check out something else while I'm in town."

"Okay, so long."

Perry offered his hand and Marvin seemed surprised. It was an awkward handshake. Then Perry got in his unmarked Ford and drove off.

Marvin lingered for a few moments, looking at the men who were handling the lines for the cruise ship. He wondered how they got that kind of work. Longshoremen were supposed to make good money, weren't they?

But he knew how it would be. *Sure kid, we'll put your name on the list. Say you were in the Navy? That'll help. What kind of ships did you serve on? What, what do you mean none? Why not? What kind of discharge did you say you have?*

He began walking downtown, heading toward the farmer's market. Maybe they would have something.

They didn't. Nor did any of the downtown fast food restaurants. He walked eight blocks to the state employment office and once again checked the 3×5 cards on the big bulletin board, but it wasn't exactly jammed to overflowing with hot prospects for the unskilled and inexperienced.

He took the bus back to Ocean Beach—gas for the Datsun was now a luxury item. The rush-hour traffic kept the bus behind schedule, but Marvin wasn't in any hurry. He calculated and then recalculated how much money he had in his checking account. Enough to take him maybe a whole month and a half into the future, if he really watched it.

He almost missed his stop, but managed to hustle off at the last moment. The bus rumbled off in a cloud of diesel exhaust, and he felt as alone and uncertain as a starlet-to-be in downtown Hollywood. He didn't want to go back to the Cota Arms, not just yet. So he started heading toward the beach, intent on a long walk.

It was late afternoon, almost sunset. The commercial section of Ocean Beach was uncrowded, with the liquor stores doing most of the trade. A big Harley blatted through an intersection, and for one cold moment Marvin thought it might be Dell. But the biker was far heavier and his hair was black as coal.

The parking lot near the municipal pier was half-full, with groups of young and not-so-young surfers and bunnies sitting on hoods, talking in groups, car stereos almost a match for the thudding surf. There was a faint tang of marijuana in the humid air.

Marvin went up the pier's concrete staircase and started the long walk down its weathered boards. The wooden railing was marked with faded stencils at regular intervals, and he read them with idiot concentration: NO OVERHEAD CASTING   NO SITTING ON RAIL . . .

"Marvin?"

He turned around and saw Kathryn trotting after him, a small plastic grocery bag dangling from her hand. He waved, suddenly glad. "Hi!"

"Hello." She was a little breathless. "I *thought* it was you!"

"What brings you out here?"

"Groceries." It took a moment for her to catch her breath. "Any luck today?"

He felt some of his troubles return, settling on his shoulders like a cloak of lead. He shrugged and smiled a little. "It's never easy finding a job."

"Well, something'll turn up." She squeezed his arm and smiled. "Besides, you're going to be a hotshot artist, remember?"

The smile came and went, like a puff of smoke. "Yeah. Almost forgot."

Kathryn kept smiling, but it gave her heart a nasty pinch to see him act this way. "Listen, you don't have any plans for dinner, do you?"

"Huh? No."

"Good, because I've made them for you." She jiggled the plastic bag. "How about it? You likee?"

The smile wasn't so tentative this time. "Me likee."

She hooked her arm through his and they fell into step.

"But what if your friend doesn't like my stuff?"

Kathryn hadn't even started getting things out of the cupboard. "Listen, you'll do *fine*. And besides, it's only a start. Here." She poured a glass of Chablis. "Make yourself comfortable. People watching me cook makes me nervous."

Marvin went into the living room and began fiddling with the stereo. Kathryn found all the parts belonging to the aluminum steamer, filled the pot with water, and turned it to boil. She washed the vegetables and started cutting them up.

I really like him a lot, Kathryn thought, but seeing him so hang-dog about this. . . .

She wondered why she wanted to push him, why she wanted anything to do with him at all. She had never been responsive to hard-luck cases before, never wanted to help anyone climb out of their problems. Even Kartismanta. Their long serious talks about their many woes hadn't seemed quite real—ersatz, really, like a pair of children reading out loud from *Death of a Salesman*.

At least up until that moment when he had broken free of the icy water and screamed her name. . . .

Was it friendship she felt for Marvin, or compassion? Or pity, if you wanted to get down and dirty. God, from what he'd told her of his life, it seemed hideous. A perpetual victim. Like this insane thing with the gas station robbery.

But the real shame of it was that there was so much potential. He was a natural-born artist; Lord knows she'd met enough artists who were just pretending—and making damn good livings. And that tiny germ of self-confidence he let her see from time to time—so responsive to the proper nuturing. She really wanted to help him. It would be a shame for Marvin to end up pittering away his life like . . .

What, old girl? Yourself?

She bit her lip and started cutting the onion into finer slices than necessary. Shit, let the boy sink on his own. Fuck him. Who the hell had ever tried to show you what you might do with your life? Who the hell had ever tried to do anything for you except con you into the sack?

Her eyes began to sting and she wiped at them with the back of her wrist.

Shit, you're a mess.

The water was boiling, filling the basket with steam. She tossed in the vegetables and put on the lid. Nature feast tonight, friends. A little nod toward the gods of nutrition and properly functioning bowels, ha ha.

The stinging wouldn't go away. She stared out the window, trying to make her mind go blank. Maybe there was some yoga-thought back there, some trick to make the eyes stop watering. The stars were beginning to come out.

Star light, star bright . . .

Get ahold of yourself, kid, before you break down into a blubbering heap of self-pity. Good thoughts only, please. Think good thoughts.

Well . . . it was warm. Cozy, even. And she wasn't alone. And Marvin had found a good station on the FM, some kind of slow, sweet jazz that sounded like a bird flying high over a lonesome forest. Good music. Seduction music . . .

She looked at the steamer and decided she really wasn't that hungry and turned off the gas. She went into the living room, where Marvin was hunched over the coffee table, leafing through an oversized book of black-and-white photographs.

Pity? she thought. No, not that. He needed her, that was all. Just as she needed someone, too.

"Hi." His smile was broad, at least until he noticed the tears on her face. "What's the matter?"

"Onions." She sat next to him and put her arms around his neck. "Just onions."

She kissed him warmly and fully, not caring what his reaction might be. It was surprise, but . . . he started to take her in his arms, the tempo of his heart quickly picking up. She pushed back, and without preamble, pulled off her tank top, then pressed herself back into him, wrapping her arms around him and saying his name.

They lay on the futon bed, exhausted, the tangled sheets bathed in moonlit tones of blue. Marvin had dozed off, and Kathryn lay with her head against his shoulder, slowly moving a fingernail through his fine spray of blond chest hairs.

She savored the moment. She liked to think this was the best part of sex, the closeness that came afterward. It was something she had almost forgotten.

Marvin stirred, getting ready to wake up. Kathryn stroked his face gently, shushing him back to sleep. He went down easily, and she liked that. She liked tending him. She liked seeing him smile.

She began retracing the aimless lines on his chest, making wide, lazy downward loops, stopping just short of his flaccid organ.

He seemed so inexperienced that at first she had thought he might be a virgin. But she told herself that could hardly be true, not in this day and age. It had to be the inexperience born of whatever hurried trysts there'd been in the backseat of a compact, or in some dorm after lights out. That sort of inexperience. He just hadn't had a real affair before.

Kathryn's eyes went wide when she heard a distant smack, followed by the tinkling of glass. She lifted her head, alert as a cat at a strange new noise. There was another smash-tinkle, and it sounded awfully close.

She got off the futon and went to the window. She could see the back alley from here, and there was a brief glimpse of a silhouette moving in the darkness, behind the garage apartment, walking around the little Datsun B-210.

Smash-tinkle.

"Marvin, wake up!" She shook him vigorously. "I think someone's trying to break in your car!"

He sat up quickly, wide-eyed, confused. She told him

what was going on, and they got dressed hurriedly. They went downstairs and out the back door, stopping at the porch. No sound. They crossed the back yard and went under the trellis of bougainvillea. There was a streetlight halfway down the alley, casting its weak light on the small piles of debris and broken glass surrounding the remains of the Datsun.

They approached it slowly, saying nothing, riveted by the sight. The windows were smashed, big shards of glass scattered over the hood and trunk and pavement. The tires had been slashed, rubber bent out flat like a Salvador Dali painting. The hood yawned open, hoses yanked and slashed, carburetor wanged with a tire iron, battery on its side with caps open. They looked through the broken windows silently, at the seats that had been thoroughly slashed, the electrical wires hanging from underneath the dash.

"Jesus," Kathryn said quietly. "Who on earth . . . ?"

But Marvin was not there to respond. She saw him disappear through the back gate, then start running up the staircase to his apartment, taking four risers with each step.

"No, Marvin! *No!*"

He disappeared around the corner of the balcony and she started running. She heard the door swing open, and there was a bang as it smacked against the wall. She ran up the stairs, across the balcony, and skidded to a halt in front of the open door.

Marvin was rock steady, wearing the expression of a man who'd just been told he'd been found guilty on all counts. The single two-hundred-watt bulb lit the scene with painful intensity, and Kathryn found it incredible that this could be the same apartment she'd visited only the other day.

The walls were festooned with wide, looping, spray-painted obscenities, the largest of which was a Day-Glo EAT ME MOY. Mattress innards were spread far and wide, a

134

cotton-ball topping for the miasma of shredded clothing, broken furniture, and splintered art supplies. The little black-and-white TV lay in a corner, loser in an argument with a steel-toed boot. And the drawings . . . ah yes, the drawings . . .

There were a few shredded pieces here and there, and the painting had been sliced up, but it looked as if vandal-fever had given way to a more thoughtful consideration of how to do things, and so the drawings and sketchpads had been collected into a central pile. It was a soggy, sodden mass, rich with the smell of drying urine.

Ghastly, Kathryn thought. So ghastly and pointless. She began stepping through the rubble, looking to see if there was anything salvageable. Marvin began a delicate walk toward the bathroom, where big porcelain shards of the broken toilet bowl lay in a puddle.

Kathryn was mesmerized by the big self-portrait. She dropped to her knees and touched it. His best work—but now, ribboned by the vertical slash of a razor, the composition had been thrown into nonsense, shifting the colors from bold to garish, the lines from a display of measured power to a scream of lunatic intensity. And she could *still* recognize the face—now as hideous and vile as the roving madman who quietly slips through bedroom windows, come to make the nightmare real.

She felt Marvin's presence behind her and slowly looked up. He was standing over her, looking at the painting, his face strangely pale, his eyes glistening with bright intensity. Kathryn felt a sudden coldness grip her heart. This was a man she knew not at all, the remotest of strangers . . . and, perhaps, entirely capable of dropping to his knees and locking his sinewy hands to her throat.

But he merely turned his back and slowly walked away. He paused in the doorway, breathing deeply of the night air, looking at the stars, and he reached up as if to massage his temple.

He collapsed abruptly, like a puppet cut from its strings. The floor trembled as if a tree had fallen against the building.

"Marvin!"

□

T H I R T E E N

The rush hour traffic on I-5 was starting to thin. A big Harley lazily outdistanced the main flow, snaking its way through the northbound lanes.

Adios, San Diego, Dell Ready thought, and fuck you very much.

His cycle banked gracefully as he slipped in front of a Chevette. He gained a little yardage and then eased back on the throttle. Dell had to keep reminding himself to take it easy. Now wasn't the time to get pulled over—having passed the city limits ten minutes ago put him in violation of bail.

He let himself grin. One fat little fuck of a bail bondsman was going to shit platinum bricks when he found out ten thou had taken a hike. But what the hell did he expect, anyway? That he'd wait for some kangaroo court to throw his ass in Folsom? Yeah, baby, sure; don't worry, I won't come in your mouth.

He shifted his weight and the Harley banked left. He eased around a yellow Volvo piloted by a brown-haired Ms. Yuppie, then increased speed so that his muffler let go with a series of racketing farts. The cycle thrummed with 1215ccs of ready power, the warm air pressed his coppery beard back flat, and his ears were filled with the roar of high speed. It'd been a long time since he'd been on the road. *Too* fucking long. Now was definitely the time for the long-dreamed-about Canadian Vacation. Screw around British Columbia, let things die down. No way the San Diego heat would take their beef all the way up there, not for some nickel-and-dime armed robbery. The bail bondsman *might* . . . but he'd taken care of little bitty problems like that before.

Canada was definitely the ticket. Big mountains, big lakes, big skies. Back to good ol' motherfucking nature. Of course, it would be sleeping on the ground and no Ramada Inns because of the way that stupid Hattstaedt operation had turned into a steaming pile of horseshit.

He grimaced, unconscious of the cycle creeping to eighty. That fucking Marvin Moy. The only piece of business left undone. It would've been nice to hear the feeb sing the song of *please oh please don't*. Dance him around until he became absolutely certain that this was it, the big one, the Grand Prize Winner of DeLuxe Permanent Hurts.

Too bad he'd missed him. He'd had to make the most of

trashing his car and crummy apartment. Sorta fun, but still nowhere near as satisfying as—

Ninety!

Dell squeezed the brakes a little and eased back on the throttle. He checked the rearview mirrors for any sign of flashing lights, heart thumping anxiously. But nothing— everything seemed okay . . . and still at the same time it didn't.

His animal alarm system had suddenly kicked in for some reason, and his hands tightened on the grips. His mouth turned down in an involuntary frown and his nostrils flared wide as he checked the rearview mirrors again, his thighs becoming sensory organs in their own right as he felt for any stray vibration in the Harley.

But the only thing out of whack was this strange pressure on his sides, as if . . . as if, well, there was some chick in the sassy seat, arms lightly wrapped around his middle. . . .

The pressure increased, becoming more real.

A hot bolt of fear sprang from his belly, making his scalp come alive with acidy beads of sweat. He felt the thin invisible arms leave his middle and slither over his forearms, moving toward his hands. And just as they started to tickle his knuckles, it began to take—for the love of sweet Jesus —it began to take *shape.*

Dell's eyes bulged from their sockets as the thing took form, coalescing from the spinnings of a thousand spider webs, becoming more and more whole with each passing second, and it was behind him too—a person becoming fleshy and real, sitting in back and reaching out to take the handgrips away.

Dell felt a strange, terrible cawing deep in his throat, and he let his hands slip from the controls so he could grab and yank at the thing's forearms. But they were hard as ma-

139

hogany, immovable as stone, and Dell felt the Harley bank as they turned onto a long, long exit ramp and he knew this was it, that they were going to crash, but the Harley only roared through the stoplight and banked sharply to the left, and Dell let out a scream as they went through the underpass and the Harley banked left again and they were tearing up the onramp and then they were on I-5 again, heading south, the Duo Glide's roar at earsplitting intensity as the speedometer crept up and up, and they weaved between the cars and Dell twisted around to see who it was and then he really began to scream, screamed as if there would never be an end to it, as if he had enough throat and lungs to go on bellowing until the end of time.

Mr. Sam hesitated when he felt the texture of the twenty-dollar bill—so damn old it was like a piece of tissue paper. Except for the Scotch tape across the middle, where a tear had been half-assed fixed. He looked at the twenty front-ways and back, then looked at the driver with equal contempt. She was one of those high school punker-cunts, hair all splayed out crazy and painted up like a dirty rainbow.

"What's the matter, little girl? Spend all your legal tender buying dope?"

"That's right, grandpa." She stared back fearlessly, jaws working on an oversized piece of bubble gum. " 'Course, if you want, you can take your gas outta the tank and I'll go somewhere else."

He made change grudgingly, carefully selecting his most gummed-up bills.

The yellow Mustang rumbled off, and Mr. Sam glanced over at his new employee. He was a tall kid, tall enough to make a basketball coach weep with joy, but he acted like he still wasn't sure whether he was right-handed or left. The kid was running his window washer across the windshield of a white Volkswagen bug—at the goddamn *self-serve*. Stupid kid didn't have enough brains to win a game of checkers playing against a two-by-four. Mr. Sam started walking toward him, smiling thinly. It was time to kick a little butt.

But midway to his destination Mr. Sam was distracted by a distant squeal of tires, and he stopped short, alert. It was one of those desperate squeals that went on endlessly, and he looked at the busy intersection two blocks up, holding his breath as he waited for the rumbling boom of colliding metal.

But the squeal only gave way to the throaty blast of a powerful engine, quickly growing louder. Then the warble of a police siren in the distant background.

Heading this way, Mr. Sam thought excitedly. Some pecker's trying to outrun the law and he's heading this way.

He stared hard at the intersection, trying to pick out the anomaly in the string of headlamps and brakelights, and was rewarded soon enough by the sight of a motorcycle rocketing down the street, banking steeply between the cars, its single headlight growing bright.

It flashed underneath the streetlamps in a blur, but Mr. Sam was able to peg it as one of those souped-up rigs like that Dell Ready owned, and holy sweet Mary if it didn't look like old Dell himself, mouth wide open and screaming like he'd just fallen off a cliff, long hair splayed wide and wild, eyes big as snuff tins. It was happening so fast there wasn't time to think about it, but there was something wrong with the picture, it didn't make sense, and what was even crazier was that Dell wasn't driving the damn thing at all, there was someone sitting in back of Dell who actually had his hands on the controls, and Mr. Sam felt his bowels turn to steamed macaroni when the big Harley banked one last time and settled its headlight beam square on his face.

A cold burst of adrenaline galvanized him instantly, but even as he turned to run he knew this was it, that he was a dead man, that the end of everything had finally come. The controls to his arms and legs were all mixed up, making him feel as if he was trying to run across a trampoline. The sound of the Harley was awesome, like a mighty Superfortress building up power for takeoff.

Mr. Sam was caught sideways by the big headlamp, knocking the air from his lungs, then collapsing his rib cage like a wicker basket. The impact slowed the machine to ninety, and it carried Mr. Sam like a rag as it hurtled toward the full-serve island. The Harley slammed into it with enough force to take the two pumps clean from their roots, and the impact sent the machine into a sideways cartwheel through the air, metal and flesh and gasoline spraying wide.

Two miles away, at Sea World, a retired attorney and his wife were riding the observation enclosure to the top of the PSA Sky Tower. It was three hundred and twenty feet straight up, the enclosure slowly rotating as it made its ascent.

They held hands as they took in the nighttime view. They were from Phoenix, on their second honeymoon, visiting the city where they had first met. She'd been a nurse then, working in the burn ward at the big naval hospital, and he a young pilot getting ready to ship out on the *Saratoga*. The Sky Tower was situated on what had been raw, undeveloped land back then, but now there were lights everywhere—in the valleys, along the coast, spread across the gentle hills like so many jewels.

The observation platform kept turning, and the big windows now afforded them a view of Point Loma, where they'd found a small apartment after a hasty courtship. The couple smiled silently.

Then, from the flat land just before the rise of Point Loma, a ball of flame boiled high into the night.

"Goodness, Paul." The woman gripped the man's hand tightly. "Look."

The man tensed and sucked in his breath. He'd seen something like this before, only it had been a PBY in a screwed-up takeoff, heavily laden with extra fuel for a long-range hop. It had been ghastly, and far too hot for the crash crew to get close enough to do any good. Even the aluminum had melted in that one.

They heard the boom, and the big windows rattled in their tracks.

What had happened to the apartment was so unreal that Kathryn had fallen into a kind of trance, but when Marvin collapsed instinct took over and she was helping him before she was aware of what she was doing.

A person passed out at Windsong Aerobics on the average of once a month. It was because of this—and for the occasional sprain and the one unforgettable heart attack—that the owner had hired a young bull-necked paramedic to give a series of first-aid lectures to the instructors. Kathryn had handled dozens of minor accidents since.

Marvin was on his side, legs folded underneath. Kathryn rolled him on his back, grabbed his arms, and pulled him out straight—a task that was like dragging a cord of firewood uphill. In the distance she could hear a radio turned high, the thump of its steady bass carrying across the night. She found the splintered remains of the desk chair and used it to provide elevation for his legs. Then she took his wrist, and the pulse was hard to find, but at least regular—he would come around in a few minutes.

Kathryn set about the task of stimulating him. She slapped

his hands. She pinched his cheeks. She went into the bathroom, found a cracked plastic glass, and filled it with water. Then she used her fingers to sprinkle it on his face and chest.

Nothing. No coughing, no stirring, nothing. She dashed the remainder of the water in his face. Still nothing. Kathryn told herself not to get panicked, that even though he'd been out longer than she was accustomed to, everything was still okay.

She went back to her apartment, where she had an old bottle of smelling salts. She'd almost thrown it away during her last housecleaning, but she still couldn't remember where she put it. She finally found it, came back, and as she climbed the stairs thought that if it didn't do the trick, she'd call the paramedics.

Just as she stepped through the door a great, rumbling boom shook the apartment. She dropped the little bottle to the floor.

It felt like a minor earthquake. She went back out to the balcony and gasped when she saw the ball of fire rising high above the black silhouettes of rooftops and palm trees.

Plane crash, she thought. My god, all the people.

One of the takeoff patterns from Lindbergh Field went directly overhead, and Kathryn remembered that awful day in 1978 when an airliner had crashed into North Park.

There was a moan from inside the apartment, and Kathryn turned around. Marvin had a hand to his head and was slowly trying to get up.

F O U R T E E N

Once she was sure he could walk, Kathryn got him to his feet and told him he was coming back to her apartment. He nodded groggily, leaning heavily on the offered shoulder. He made no comment on the column of smoke and orange sparks in the eastern sky, or on the cacophony of wavering sirens.

They made it to her apartment, and although she hadn't intended it—she was only trying to get him to the bathroom—he collapsed on the futon bed. She tried to get him up, but he was already in deep sleep. So she took off his running shoes and pulled the sheet up over his legs.

She went into the living room, turned the radio on, and switched over to the AM all-news channel. Nothing about the explosion yet. She took out a half-smoked joint and started to light up, then realized it was the last thing she wanted. After a day like this she needed the heavy-duty stuff. She found the bottle of cheap rum a friend had brought back from his last trip to Mexico, and made do with a can of Diet Coke.

Halfway through the drink she turned up the radio. ". . . and four units are now on the scene of a spectacular service station fire at the corner of Voltaire and Mason in Ocean Beach. Witnesses say an automobile traveling at a high rate of speed went out of control and slammed into the fuel pumps at the Chevron station, setting off an explosion that has claimed at least four lives. . . ."

Kathryn was relieved it hadn't been something as horrible as a plane crash. Then it dawned on her that the address was familiar; in fact, Marvin had given it to her when he wanted her to call the police.

It wasn't a Chevron station at all—it was that junky little place where he used to work. . . .

She shuddered. If Marvin cursed his luck tomorrow, she would tell him he wasn't so unlucky after all.

Kathryn took a stiff pull at her drink, thinking back to the night of the robbery. And of Marvin banging at her door, wide-eyed and sweaty, telling her that he knew it was being robbed, that he hadn't seen or heard anything but just *knew*.

Marvin woke at eight. His sleep had been dreamless, but now, as he began to recognize the interior of Kathryn's bedroom, his fuzzed mind told him he was on the threshold of some wonderfully erotic dream.

But the morning light was too bright, the bed too solid and real . . . and a picture of what had happened to his apartment came to his mind, as sharp and clear as a full-page layout in *Life* magazine.

He waited for the pall of gloom and despair to settle on his shoulders, but . . . nothing came. In fact, the reverse seemed to be in order. He felt great. Never mind that all his possessions were trashed. Never mind that his art work was ruined. What mattered now . . . was the memory of what had finally taken place on this bed last night. . . .

He felt ready to take on the world.

Marvin padded out of bed and into the living room, saw Kathryn in the kitchenette working the spatula in a skillet of scrambled eggs.

"Hi there."

"Good morning, Marvin." Her smile was as broad and cheerful as the light outside. "How're you feeling?"

"Never better."

Kathryn told him there was orange juice in the Frigidaire, and he helped himself as she ladled the eggs onto two china plates. There were croissants in the oven and some hippy-dippy natural jam from Sunshine Grocer's. They took everything into the living room to eat off the coffee table.

"Think you should call the police?" Kathryn asked.

"About last night?" Marvin thought of Sergeant Perry's card in his wallet. "Maybe. I don't know. It's not going to change anything, that's for sure."

"But whoever did it . . . do you think it was that biker guy?"

Marvin was about to say *Who else?* but something about Dell tried to push itself into his mind. Something about that Duo Glide of his. . . . He ended up shrugging.

"But if that man's out to get you . . ."

"I'm not worried." The words were out before he'd thought about it, and Marvin was surprised. But shit, the fact was he *wasn't* worried. Somehow Dell Ready was just not a problem anymore.

"Besides," Marvin said, "the important thing is to figure out what I'm going to do next. No use crying over spilt milk, you know. I've got to get on with it."

"Think you can salvage some of those drawings?"

"Well . . . maybe if there's a good enough Xerox machine somewhere, something could be done." He smiled. It was a given that he couldn't take the piss-saturated drawings to a gallery. "Anyway, I was planning on starting a new series. That is, if you don't mind a little modeling."

She smiled back.

"But until then, I've got to find a job. And clean up that apartment."

They talked about other things while they ate, but inside Kathryn was doing glad somersaults. Such a change from last night at the pier, when she had found him so whipped and downtrodden. Now he was a personable, confident young man, picking himself up and getting ready to go back in the ring.

He's really going to make it, she thought. He's not going to let them keep him down.

She told him she didn't have anything to do all morning; her class didn't start until two-thirty. She could help him with the want ads, drive him wherever he needed to go. Then, quite innocently, "Oh, I don't know how I forgot. You missed some real excitement last night."

"How's that?"

"There was some terrible accident at that place you used to work. A car smashed into one of the fuel pumps and there was this tremendous explosion. I could see the fire from . . . here . . ." Kathryn let the words trail off, croissant halfway to her mouth.

Marvin had that same strange look on his face, that same stonelike expression he'd worn just before passing out last night. And he'd gone deathly pale, too. Kathryn was sure he was on the verge of another collapse.

But he didn't. He got up shakily, and headed toward the bathroom.

The reporters and television cameramen were long gone, but there were still quite a few onlookers standing behind the fluttering yellow tape of the police line. Marvin and Kathryn stared at the scene silently.

It reminded Kathryn of pictures of Hiroshima. Hattstaedt's Sup'r Serv was now blackened and almost flat, and what was left of the fuel pumps looked like charred cornstalks. The service station building was gone, save for the rear wall, half as tall as it'd once been. Two cars had been parked in the service bays, and it was impossible to tell the make of their burnt hulks. Firemen used pikes to shift through the rubble.

It was, fortunately, an intersection with few businesses. There was a liquor store and a waterbed showroom across the street, and their plate glass windows had been blown in. Even now workmen were fitting in huge sheets of plywood. The closest palm trees had been denuded of their fronds, making them look strangely forlorn.

"It must have been awful," Kathryn said. "The driver of that car must've been drunk out of his mind."

"He wasn't drunk." Marvin's face was impassive, except where a muscle rippled at his cheek. "And he wasn't driving a car."

149

"Huh?"

But Marvin was shouldering his way through the crowd, heading away from the scene.

"Marvin?"

He jogged across the street, gaining speed, beginning to run.

"Marvin!"

Kathryn started to follow but saw him duck down an alley. She backtracked to her Volvo, started it up, and went after him.

It was almost sunset when she parked against the beach sidewalk. She got out, took off her sandals, and tossed them through the driver's window. Then she walked across the sidewalk, stepped over the wall, and began trudging through the powdery sand.

Marvin was sitting atop the basalt jetty, staring at the ocean. A pelican hovered just beyond the surf line, looking for prey. Kathryn wondered how long Marvin had been sitting there—the last time she had checked the beach was at least an hour ago.

The pelican folded it wings and plummeted down, hitting the water with a small burst of spray.

She'd been looking for him all day, and only once, when she stopped to grab a quick burger at a sidewalk deli, had she wondered why she was searching for him so frantically.

Because he's come so close to getting his act together you can't let him fall apart now. Whatever it was that upset him about that gas station, you've got to find him fast and make him see that it doesn't have anything to do with how he should live the rest of his life.

But as she approached, she wondered if that was entirely true. As she had been looking down those alleys, the baking interior of the Volvo making the sweat pour down in tor-

150

rents, hadn't there been a wrenching in her guts when she thought about her apartment yawning emptily before her?

Three miles out a slender powerboat pounded northward, kicking up a roostertail, the thrumming of its engine carried by the breeze.

She had not yet reached the jetty when Marvin suddenly turned and looked at her. It surprised Kathryn, but she smiled as she started climbing the jetty, arms lifted high as she stepped from one uneven surface to another. Marvin did not rise to greet her, but his smile seemed friendly enough. She put her hand on his shoulder. "You okay?"

He nodded, then looked away.

"Mind if I join you?"

She felt his shoulders rise a quarter-inch. The indifference made Kathryn's chest go cold. *He's leaving me*, she thought uneasily, but she made herself smile as she sat on the boulder.

Marvin had a handful of pebbles, and was tossing them toward the water one by one.

"Are you still thinking about the gas station?"

He nodded.

She had a speech half-prepared. "You really should stop it, you know. You aren't responsible for that accident." She leaned close, putting her hands on his shoulders, "There's no reason for you to feel any . . . well, *guilt*, or whatever it is that's bothering you."

He turned to look at Kathryn, and she saw that the muscle near his right eye was twitching. "But I do."

"But *why?*"

He looked away, squinting at the red sun. He sighed. "It's kind of like . . . I had a dream about it. A real strange dream. I mean, I didn't remember it when I woke up, but when you told me what happened I started to . . . well, parts of it began to come back. And it wasn't like I was

151

remembering a regular dream. This was more like I had actually *been* there."

She felt a strange sense of relief. "That doesn't mean anything, Marvin. Your mind's been worked up about that place, that's all. With that robbery, and your getting fired . . . and everything, I mean, is it any wonder? So when you heard about the accident, your subconscious just started making connections on its own. Don't you see?"

Doubt crossed his face, and he turned away.

"Marvin, it isn't doing you any good to worry about it like this." Kathryn felt a tiny glow of triumph—the situation was going to come under control. She knew it. "You've got to put it out of your mind. Get it behind you."

"But . . ."

"But what? Forget about it. Please."

He looked at her again, and his face seemed different. More grown-up, somehow; and in an unpleasant sort of way. "But it was so much like that time when I saw the robbery at the station that night."

Kathryn sat back, confused, no answer at the ready. "Oh?"

"Remember? Remember when I came to your apartment, banging on the door like—"

"Yes," she said quickly.

"It was like that. Like I was *there*." He grimaced and looked away. "Kathryn, I . . . I don't know how to explain it. I've never tried explaining to anyone else before. Not even myself, really, but . . ."

He let the words trail off. Kathryn stared at him raptly, trying to think of something to say, sure that if she could come up with something—*anything*—she would veer his mind from this . . . senseless tack.

But her lips would not move.

"It's been going on since I was a little boy," he said quietly. "Being able to . . . see things in other places. Like

I was watching some kind of movie. Or more like I was there—but invisible, you know? Just standing there and . . . looking."

She took his hand. "Listen, Marvin. That's . . . interesting, and weird, and whatever else you want to call it. But, I mean, so what? So you can see things. That still doesn't make you responsible for what happened last night, does it?"

He shook his head, and Kathryn felt a coldness touch her heart.

"But *how*, Marvin? Why?"

"I don't know!"

He stood up and started walking away, stepping lightly from one boulder to another. Kathryn scrambled up and started going after him, but her foot went into a crevice and she sprawled to all fours, crying out.

Marvin turned. "Kathryn?" He rushed back. "Are you all right?"

His heart wrenched sideways when she looked up—her face was strained, desperate, on the verge of tears. He went to his knees and took her in his arms.

"Let's go home, Marvin." She was crying, hiccuping. "Please, darling. Let's just go home."

F I F T E E N

Kathryn picked up the breakfast dishes and went into the kitchen, humming. This was what? The eighth breakfast with Marvin? She backtracked through the days and discovered that was about right.

She took the plastic dishpan from the lower cupboard and put it in the sink, turned on the hot water spigot, and squeezed in some Lemon Fresh Joy. She rarely washed dishes in the morning—preferring to leave it as an after-dinner chore—but lately she'd been cleaning up after each meal.

Not that she felt she was getting into a domestic routine. It was just . . . nice.

She scraped off the dishes into a plastic grocery bag underneath the sink. Marvin had gone to the corner to pick up the morning paper so he could look through the want ads. But that little ritual would be over soon, and if there were no job interviews, then it would be time for the beach. Or maybe a drive over to Balboa Park to see one of the museums. Or a visit to Old Town, for a long walk amongst the tourists. Maybe they'd even splurge and have a couple of piña coladas at one of the outdoor Mexican cafés, getting pleasantly tight as they listened to the serenade of strolling musicians. She'd done these things many times in the course of her years in San Diego—but with Marvin it seemed as if she'd just moved to someplace new and fantastically exotic.

She had already suggested that he just quit looking for work and concentrate on his painting. After all, he was moved in now, the rent was basically free, and her teaching brought in enough for the essentials. But he had flatly refused, saying it wouldn't be right, and although Kathryn thought his attitude rather quaint, she couldn't help but be pleased by his growing confidence and self-esteem.

She set the dishes in the rack to dry and dumped the dishwater into the drain. Marvin's assurance certainly carried over into the bedroom, too; that was for sure. It was so different from that sweet, tentative lovemaking of the first time. Not that it was bad—far from it—it was just that . . . sometimes he acted like another person, a madman almost, and when he really got going it was all she could do to hang onto him breathlessly, stunned by his power, her mind working like some kind of overloaded electrical relay, snapping on and off and spewing sparks, spinning her off into some great velvety void.

She dried her hands with the dish towel and noticed they were trembling.

Another person, she thought. That was an odd way of looking at it, but . . . sometimes she'd come up behind him while he was working on a drawing at that cheap drafting table they'd bought at the Salvation Army, and he'd whip his head around as if it was on a spring, startled, looking at her with eyes that were at once frightened and hostile. His expression would instantly change to warm friendliness, but . . .

Other times he would be staring at nothing—at the beach, in the apartment, wherever—and as seemingly preoccupied as if he were playing an entire game of chess inside his head. His face would look different then. Hard. Flat. Alien, even. And she would feel her stomach go all buttery when she thought about him banging at her door, telling her he *knew* Hattstaedt's was being robbed, or that (as the newspaper later bore out) it was a motorcycle that had crashed into the gas pumps.

But they hadn't discussed it. It had become a forbidden topic, somehow. That afternoon on the jetty had been the first and last time they talked about . . . whatever. Which was fine with Kathryn. She was more than willing to let this particular sleeping dog lie undisturbed.

But still, Kathryn could not help but wonder. . . .

She had never thrown away a book since high school, and her library had grown to respectable proportions. A few shelves reflected her occult/paranormal phase, and she found herself drawn to those unused volumes whenever Marvin was away.

The ones she looked at first were of the modern, "scientific" variety. These were usually well-indexed, and it was easy to find references to "Out of Body Experiences"—or OOBEs, as it was inevitably acronymed. There were even discussions of "remote viewing"—phenomena where a person could project their mind to a distant location. She read of one experiment where nine researchers drove to different parts of San Francisco, and the "psychically gifted" subject attempted to describe where they had gone. He got six out of nine.

A nice trick, Kathryn thought, but there were others who only needed grid coordinates in order to get the juices flowing. Give them a latitude and longitude, and they'd describe that location with surprising accuracy. One man even went so far as an island in the Indian Ocean, where his "second body" reported that he had heard people speaking French. It turned out to be a former colony. There were dark hints that these talents were being exploited by the superpowers for military purposes.

But these passages were unsatisfying to Kathryn—she knew something of scholarly research and controlled experimentation, and these writings bordered on quackery. The grainy photographs of the researchers were enough to put her off, anyway. Frumpy women with odd hairstyles and strange little grins. Intense but furtive-looking men who wore shirts that Kathryn swore were pajama tops. Doctors all—but of what it was never said. And each "associated" with "major universities" and "world-renowned centers of learning."

What Kathryn found vastly more interesting was the stuff that made no pretense at rationalism. And she found that projection of the soul at will was an extremely ancient feature in folk mythology. Shamans in all cultures were commonly attributed with the ability to leave their bodies and soar to distant locations, sometimes to strike down an enemy. In the Book of Daniel a prophet was "in Susa the capital, which is in the province of Elam; and I saw the vision, and I was at the river Ulai." The battle plans that a

157

Syrian king hatched in his innermost council were compromised because "Elisha the prophet that is in Israel telleth the king of Israel the words that thou speakest in thy bedchamber."

The literature was rife with stories of second-selves, "subtle" bodies, and "perispirits" that could be seen in a different location than its owner. There was the Gaelic *samhla*, whose semi-transparent appearance was evidence that the shadow-soul was on the loose. The Norwegians had the *vardøger* and *fylgja*. The ancient Greeks the *daemon*. There was the *fetch* of Western Europe. The *waft*, *task*, and *fye* of Britain. The German *judel* and *doppelganger*. Even the Catholic Church accepted what it called "bilocation," although it was a talent reserved for individuals of the strictest piety. And the Egyptians spoke of the *ka*, a double created at its owner's birth . . . and which was left behind in the tomb when the *ba*—the soul—took its leave.

Tales of the appearance of a person's double were common, even among the famous. Guy de Maupassant reported that his double frequently sat opposite him at the writing desk, dictating stories. Shelley's double was seen by Byron and others when the poet was known to be elsewhere. Queen Elizabeth I saw her double immediately before her death, looking "pallid, shrivelled, and wan." Goethe described how he had been riding in Alsace, intent on visiting a sweetheart, when something tugged at his memory. Years before, after having visited the same girl, he had seen an apparition coming toward him on horseback, a man who looked remarkably like himself but was obviously older, dressed in gray and green . . . which was what he was wearing now . . .

Kathryn didn't know what to make of it. She wasn't even sure she *wanted* to make anything of it. After all, everything else was just as fine as it could be. This other stuff was just . . . a wild card seesawing through their relationship, and if she could just look away, she knew she could handle it. She wanted to take the books down to the city dump.

She slung the dish towel back over its rack, looking out the kitchenette window, which was eye level with the leafy top of an avocado tree thirty feet away. Beyond that was the two-story garage/apartment where Marvin used to live, then the jumbled rectangles of homes and apartments, power and telephone lines, palm trees both short and tall. It was a view that had once filled her with a vague unease, almost as if it were the view from a prison window.

But she told herself that times had finally changed. Everything was going to work out fine. Just *fine*.

The day's expedition only turned out to be a trip to the municipal pier, but that was fine with Kathryn. It was a beautiful day, and she cared not at all that Marvin hadn't found anything interesting in the want ads. The air was clean and fresh, the seagulls picturesque, the smell from the pierside fish-and-chips stand delicious.

"Kathryn?"

"Hmmm?"

"Listen . . . I've been thinking about going back to school again."

"Oh. Oh, really!" She stopped, beaming up at him. "I think that's fantastic! A wonderful idea. When are you going to enroll?"

He grinned easily. "I don't know. I just decided to go back, that's all. What I need is to figure out how I can afford it, how I can set it up."

"Oh."

"And I need you to help me figure it out." He took her arm and started walking again. "After all, you're the one

159

who showed me that if you wanted something bad enough, you could get it."

Kathryn smiled ruefully. *Me? I showed him that?* She held his arm tightly, leaning against him, and began thinking. Scholarships? Hmmm. A straight-out loan? Hmmm. Maybe show his pictures to some kind of arts council, see if they might cough up something?

A few yards ahead a seagull floated down, wings curved and still, tail feathers fanned wide. It landed on the railing and started making a small business of getting its wings properly nestled.

"How about your parents?" Kathryn found herself saying. "Don't you think they could help?"

He snorted. "Out of the question. They don't care if I'm alive or dead."

She looked at his profile. "I'm sure you don't mean that."

"Honestly, Kate . . ." He shook his head. "They wrote me off a long time ago."

Once again she pulled him to a halt. They were abreast of the seagull, and it opened its wings and started grabbing air, pulling itself upward.

"Marvin, listen to me. Time changes things. It heals wounds, just like they say. The hard edges get rounded off."

"Yeah, but—"

"You're their *son*, for God's sake. And I'm sure they're just as eager as you are to bury the hatchet."

"Is that the way it was . . . for you?"

Kathryn hesitated, looking away. "Yes. There was a lot of bitterness between me and my folks, but . . . we got over it." She looked back at Marvin. "Go to them. Please. Believe me, you'll regret it if you don't."

Marvin was looking at the weathered planks, thinking. Kathryn searched his face intently, wondering if he had sensed the white lie about her reconciliation with her parents. But it was for a good cause, and not just because he needed help in going back to school—she *knew* he'd regret it one day. She knew that very well.

They went that afternoon, Kathryn's Volvo working its way up the steep inclines into Mission Hills. Kathryn was iridescent in her black-and-aquamarine aerobics outfit; she intended to go to her class after dropping Marvin off. Marvin was stone silent, save for the occasional mumbled direction.

Mission Hills was an older area of the city, and expensive. Not that it was Beverly Hills—most homes were medium-sized, set on meager parcels of land—but even the most modest of two-bedrooms started at a quarter of a million. Kathryn knew this, and was mildly surprised that Marvin was a product of these upper-middle-class means, but she was stunned when he directed her to stop in front of an honest-to-God *mansion*.

Marvin got out and slammed the door. Kathryn couldn't take her eyes off the house. It was Spanish, two-and-a-half stories, with shade trees dotting its incredible half-acre of lawn. Marvin leaned in the window. "Well, wish you were coming with me."

It took some effort to draw her eyes away from the house. Rich kid, she thought, Marvin Moy's a rich kid.

"No . . . no, really." She put the car in gear. "If you want me to meet your parents sometime, that'll be fine. But now's not the time."

His smile came and went. "Okay. So long."

He turned and started walking up the driveway. Kathryn watched him for a moment, wondering how things would go. She'd asked if he shouldn't call first, but he'd quickly shaken his head.

She sighed and drove away from the curb. Ten minutes to the start of her class, but at least it was only two miles from here.

A rich kid—how about that?

He couldn't decide whether to use the front door or go around to the kitchen. The kitchen had been his customary entrance when he was little, but now the front door would probably be better. He began walking toward the house, wishing that he *was* still little, instead of a grown—

What? Fuckup? Don't think like that anymore. Don't let them intimidate you. You're meeting these people on your terms, remember? Just keep—

Marvin concentrated on walking up the pathway, counting the intervals between the hidden garden lights. But his eyes kept flickering to the house—it seemed much bigger than he remembered. He was halfway up the path when the front door swung wide, and there was Mom, one hand on the knob, the other at her throat, eyes a little wide and faraway.

Marvin continued walking, making his lips form into a smile, wondering what was going to be his opening line after having not said so much as boo in two years.

"Hi, Mom."

She was a tall woman, with the same fine blond hair as her son. But while Marvin's features might best be described as bland, hers were sharp and aristocratic. Still, there was no smile of recognition or welcome. She merely continued with that look of vague puzzlement. "I knew you were coming, Marvin. I . . . . I've been thinking about it all morning."

He shrugged and smiled. "Well, here I am."

She pulled the door wide and motioned for him to come inside. It was cool and airy, and looked quite ready for a photographer from *House Beautiful*. They went into the room his mother had always insisted on calling the library, although Marvin could not help but think of it as the TV room. The old RCA console had given way to a Mitsubishi projection screen, alive with the end-credits of "General Hospital." A half-empty highball glass was in its customary spot, handy by the Barcalounger. His mother picked it up.

"You are staying for dinner, aren't you?"

"Uh, yes. I mean, sure. If you want me to."

That dreamy, puzzled look left her face momentarily, long enough for her sharp features to become even sharper. "Of course we do, Marvin. After all, you're family."

He bobbed his head quickly, eager to avoid a confrontation.

"I'll just go to the kitchen and tell Carla to set another place. The intercom's on the fritz again."

"I'll be right here, Mom."

He heard his mother's footsteps ticking down the inlaid tile of the hallway. He wanted to follow her, or at least look over the house. But his status had changed, somehow. He was more like a guest. How he wished it otherwise! How he wished he were a little boy again, in his own room, hiding under the covers—

Hold it, hold it! Steady down—

He looked around the room. Everything was exactly the same, except for the imposing Mitsubishi. His picture was still on the mantel, right next to the picture of his sister Elizabeth—dark-haired, lovely, smiling. . . .

He remembered the day that picture had been taken. It was her fifteenth birthday—a wonderful garden party, a gala with almost a hundred people in attendance. Marvin had had his twelfth birthday just a few months before, and it hadn't been quite so elaborate. Matter of fact, it had just been a cake from the bakery section of the supermarket,

163

served up after dinner, but then Liz was the bright one, the shining star; straight As, captain of the drill team, vice president of the student council. . . .

The photograph was painfully radiant—all the more so because Liz had had less than a year to live when it was taken. She had drowned in a sailing accident, just a few months shy of her sixteenth birthday, casting a pall over the house that had never really lifted.

His mother came back into the room, smiling, highball freshened. "I called your father, too. I told him we were having a special guest tonight."

"How is Dad?"

"Oh, you know. The center of the entire universe is his terribly important wheeling and dealing. Have a seat, why don't you."

They both arranged themselves on a small sofa, looking at each other from opposite ends.

His mother made an effort at a bright, cheerful face. She was good at brave, noble efforts. "Well, how have you been getting along, son?"

He grinned foolishly. *Oh, you know how it is, Mom. Pretty damn busy being a fuckup.* He grimaced. *Easy! Easy! Don't let it start!* He spread his hands and started to say something, but . . . but watched his mother slowly place her face in her hand—her free hand, the other one still had the glass —and begin a delicate sobbing.

"Hey, Mom. Hey . . ."

She cried. And cried. It was what Marvin had dreaded the most. He sidled over and put an arm around her hesitantly. "Hey, Mom . . . come on, it's not that bad. Really . . ."

She cried harder, shuddering so much the highball started to slop on the blue carpet. Marvin patted her awkwardly,

164

desperately. "I'm sorry, Mom, really, please don't cry like this, I'm sorry, I'm sorry . . ."

"Why haven't you *called*?" Her face was strained and ugly. "Why haven't you let us know where you *are*?"

"Mother, please—"

"We didn't know if you were alive or dead! Do you hear me, Marvin? *Alive or dead!*"

"Oh, Mother, I'm sorry so sorry please, Mother, stop crying . . ."

His insides rumbled with nausea. His pretense at being a grown-up man was all over now, all washed up, shown up for the rickety thing that it was, for his mother's tantrum had worked a dreadful kind of magic, making him feel exactly as he had when he was a little boy, insides twisted into a thousand knots as she wept over the broken vase or the hidden *Mad* magazine or the grades on his report card or any of a thousand other things that had made her so desperately unhappy with him.

But it ended at last, with Mrs. Moy gently pushing her son away and straightening up. She took a quick pull off the highball, face contorted and pinched, tears streaming down her cheeks. "Oh, really." She brushed at her cheek, hard. "Oh, I must look a mess. You've got to excuse me for a moment, Marvin." She got up and hurried out of the room.

Marvin felt like using the bathroom . . . to puke out his ever-loving guts. But he got up and began pacing, and it seemed to help. He felt itchy and restless. He knew his mother would be a long time freshening up. He opened the door and went out into the big hallway. Even though the house was stuffed with furniture and rugs and paintings, it seemed empty and unlived-in, like a landmark home, run by the Park Service.

165

He walked up the staircase quietly. There were new curtains on the window at the top of the landing, but everything else looked pretty much the same. And there was no unlived-in feeling up here—there was a definite presence . . . albeit one that struck Marvin as cold and unfriendly.

He went down the hallway to his old room and opened the door. It had been converted into some kind of sewing room. A long folding table stood where his bed used to be, and his old chest of drawers was gone. His desk had been moved to the far wall, and it was piled high with an assortment of McCall's and Butterick sewing patterns. He opened the closet and saw that it was devoid of so much as a coathanger.

He lingered, trying to imagine the room as it had been, trying to pick up some faint echo of familiarity. But even the dimensions of the room seemed different, and the air itself was as close and still as a tomb's. There was nothing of himself here anymore.

Except, of course, for the window . . .

He moved toward it slowly, telling himself that he only wanted it open in order to relieve the stuffiness. He leaned over the sewing table and flipped the latch, grunting as he pushed up on the inner sash. A warm gust of air made the curtains rise.

Marvin stood back, smiling, remembering.

The view was something else, the kind in which you could lose yourself, there was so much going on. Planes taking off from the airport. Ships moving into the harbor. The rise of the tall office buildings downtown. He'd spent whole afternoons staring out, letting his mind float and roam and touch where it would, until the shadow of Point Loma lengthened across the harbor and stars began to dust the sky.

Marvin sighed. He supposed it was time to go looking for his mother, but . . . he moved the sewing machine out of the way. It was a new Singer with a keypad for two dozen stitch patterns, already coated with a fine layer of dust.

He parked his haunch on the table and peered out the window, the bright mid-afternoon sun making him squint. The din of I-5 was a distant roar, carried uncertainly by the breeze. Out in the harbor, a huge aircraft carrier—perhaps the *Ranger* or the *Constellation*—was slowly maneuvering into a berth at North Island. A flash of bright metal caught his eye, and he felt a small rush of pleasure when he recognized it as a commercial airliner, inbound for Lindbergh Field. He had always enjoyed watching airplanes best, especially when they were coming in for a landing. Then the great things moved with such leisurely majesty that they seemed as wonderful as any fairy-tale dragon.

Marvin tried to pick out the airliner's insignia, but its body was mostly unpainted aluminum and the markings were obscured by the reflected sun. A thin contrail ribboned out behind the starboard wing, then was gone . . . *and he saw how the pilot and co-pilot were erect in their seats; silent and intent in the cramped cockpit. The flaps were fully extended, the wheels down and locked. Steady on the glide slope, the runway's centerline perfectly aligned. The pilot eased the throttles forward, goosing the airspeed back up to a hundred and forty knots. The runway gently seesawed, slowly floating upward. The threshold lights passed underneath, then the big painted chevrons of the overrun, and finally the runway numbers. The skid marks of the touchdown area came up rapidly, and the pilot pulled back into the flare. There was one bump and then another, and the spoilers popped up. The pilot made ready to engage the thrust reversers.*

Marvin sat back and smiled, watching the silvery aircraft

roll out. The trick hadn't always been this easy; in fact, it had come amazingly easy this time. Effortlessly, really.

When he was a little boy things had been different. The images had been fuzzy and vague and often nonsensical, not really coming into sharp focus until he was thirteen. Then the change had been as sudden and confusing as his deepening voice; suddenly there'd been power enough to read the oil temp gauge inside a trucker's cab. It was good; he'd been thrilled; but . . . it'd been a disastrous year otherwise.

Marvin looked at the tall stand of eucalyptus that de-marked the limits of the back yard. Their shadows were beginning to touch the pool's apron.

He had loved his sister very much and was sure she had loved him, too. She always tried to help him with his homework, and even took him on an occasional sailing or picnic outing with her friends. But sometimes she'd get impatient and start calling him a doofus, or even some of the words their father used like *goddamn fuckup*, and Marvin couldn't help but wonder about the way she looked at him after she'd told their parents of her latest high school triumph, a look that had a little something more mixed in with it than pride.

Sometimes she acted as if she hated him, other times she was his best friend, and at still other times . . . like when they were in the pool, playing underwater tag, splashing at each other, things would suddenly come to a stop, and she would look at him in a completely new sort of way, one that he couldn't name. And he couldn't help but notice how different she was from him, how she was short, how her complexion was olive—but altogether quite as lovely as a model in one of his mother's fashion magazines. Oh, yes . . . Then she would splash him again and climb from the pool, giggling.

Sometimes, at night, when he'd be heading to their shared bathroom, she would suddenly walk out, nightgown on, and look at him in that same way . . . then quickly walk off to her room, and he would stare at how the graceful lines of her back flowed down to the growing swell of hips.

There were nights when he lay awake, senses tuned so sharply he could hear her in the room down the hall, turning in her bed, breathing, maybe having as much trouble getting to sleep as he. He would want to . . . touch himself, then. But he knew it was wrong, remembering his father's lectures on how such a thing would be terrible and vile, and he would resolve to be good, staring at the ceiling until it began to lighten with the first streaks of dawn.

But he couldn't help the dream. It had only been just that one time, and you really couldn't help a dream . . . but oh Lord it had been just as he imagined. She had fought at first, just as he knew she would, but it was only pretend-resistance, for she took him into her arms soon enough and then it became something more than he had dared imagine, much more.

You dirty little bastard you do—

Only that one time, but he had awoken feeling filthy and shameful. It was a terrible thing to have wanted something like that—

You dirty little bastard you do that again and I'll tell

—because it was a sin, one of those mortal sins, something that his father said was the worst of all abominations, and he went off to the shower, wanting only to scrub and scrub—

I'll tell Daddy! You hear me? I'll tell Daddy and he'll kill you!

—himself until he felt clean and whole again, and able to look his own family in the eye.

But he had never felt good about his sister again, because she drowned shortly thereafter, during the big Junior Division Regatta. All her friends and all her parents' friends had attended the funeral, and everyone agreed it was the most terrible of accidents, that it was such a pity none of the racing officials got to her in time, that they just couldn't see how it could have happened. But she had just slipped, Marvin knew, just slipped overboard and gotten confused and panicked. Even now, all these years later, it was so easy to close his eyes and know that she had just lost her footing when she went forward to untangle the jib from a hangup on the stay, that's all. True, it was peculiar that she had *backed* her way to the bow, staring all the while at the cockpit with a look on her face like she was trying to remember how to scream, but the deck was wet and the boat was just too small for someone to stand up in without it getting wobbly, and she became entangled in the jib before she knew what was going on and it panicked her, just plain panicked her, all those yards and yards of white Dacron flapping and popping in that stiff breeze like a string of firecrackers, and the more she pushed and flailed the more it just seemed to wrap itself around her, until she just finally . . .

S I X T E E N

"Marvin?"

His mother was in the doorway, an uncertain look on her freshly scrubbed face. "Are you . . . ready to come back downstairs?"

"Oh, sure. Of course."

They went down together, saying nothing, the silence tense and awkward. He followed her into the butler's pantry, where the liquor supplies were kept, and she asked him if he wanted anything. He shook his head.

She opened the small refrigerator and pulled out the automatic ice-maker's bin. "I hope you'll forgive me that little scene in the library." She looked pained as she dropped cubes into a glass. "But it's just that, well, you've been out of touch for so long. Not that I can really blame you, Marvin, with all the bad blood between you and your father, but I mean, *really*. Couldn't you have shown *me* a little more consideration?"

"Mom, I'm sorry, I—"

"Oh, no, no, no. Don't trouble yourself. It's nothing for you to get worried about." She twisted the cap off a bottle of Johnnie Walker. "I'm your mother, after all. I understand." She poured two fingers' worth and picked up the glass. "Come on, dear. Let's go back to the library, shall we?"

They went back down the hallway, and Mrs. Moy arranged herself on the small sofa, raising her eyebrows in surprise when she saw that her son was still standing in the doorway.

"Do you, Mother? Do you really understand?"

"Of *course* I do." She looked genuinely shocked. "I'm your *mother*. I *love* you. Remember that always, son. Even in spite of your . . . in spite of your failure."

Marvin stared at the floor, feeling his stomach roll. "Yes, of course," he said quietly.

She put on a brave smile. "Oh, darling, please don't look so guilty. After all, you're a young man, and young men are always so vain and self-centered. You'll grow out of it."

There was the sound of a car pulling up the driveway, then the distant rumbling of the automatic garage door sliding up its rails.

"That has to be your father," Mrs. Moy said. "Please have a seat, dear. You make me uncomfortable standing there like that."

Marvin did as he was told. His mother leaned over and, smiling, gave him a pat on the leg. "Don't be upset, darling. Self-pity is really so unbecoming. Now, let's try and look cheerful for your father, shall we?"

Marvin nodded dumbly, balling his fists so tightly the fingernails made little marks in his palms.

Mr. Moy came walking into the room, hat clasped in one hand, newspaper and briefcase in the other. He was a short man with big tortoiseshell glasses. He was balding, but kept it long and curly in the back, and had a goatee that had become grayer since Marvin's last visit.

"Well, well," he said. He was looking at Marvin as if he were a suspicious piece of merchandise. "Well, well, well."

Marvin stood, forcing a smile. "Hello, Dad."

"Yeah." His father went over to the bar and poured himself a Jack Daniels and branch, keeping his eyes on Marvin the whole while. He took a sip of his drink, then reached into the folds of his flannel jacket and withdrew a thick cigar. He made a show of lighting it up. There was nothing but dead silence in the room. Mr. Moy sat heavily in a leather wingbacked chair, puffing at his cigar. He took a sip of his drink and sighed. His thick glasses made his eyes look gigantic, distorted.

"Well, Marv. What kind of trouble you in now?"

There was a pause of about three seconds before Mrs. Moy spoke up. "Really, Henry. Do you have to take that kind of attitude?"

"What?" He was honestly surprised.

Mrs. Moy narrowed her blue eyes. "Marvin is our *son*. If he needs our help—"

"Okay, okay." He sat forward and started squirming out of his jacket. "It's just that the boy hasn't exactly been what you would call a great source of pride lately." He tossed

173

the jacket on a thick footstool and leaned back in his chair. He turned his thick glasses toward Marvin. "When was the last time you were here, kid?"

"I guess . . . I guess a couple of years ago."

"Couple years." He chewed the cigar thoughtfully. "Yeah, that sounds right."

"But I called—"

"Yeah, back when you got kicked out of the Navy. I remember."

A stout young Mexican girl came into the room wearing a shy but earnest grin. "Please, the dinner is on the table."

Marvin could not help but notice his mother lifting her chin as she turned to the girl. "Thank you, Carla. We'll be right along."

The girl left. Marvin guessed that she was an illegal, which his father had once told him were the best. Cheap, and no backchat.

Cloris Moy rose, but her husband remained seated, eyes still fixed on Marvin. He took the cigar from his mouth. "So what're you doing now, Marv? Fry cook somewhere? Pumping gas?"

"Now *really*, Henry." There was a note of anger in her voice. "Can't we at least *act* civilized?"

"All right, okay!" He grunted as he rose from the chair.

Marvin followed his parents into the dining room. There were two big arched windows, offering up a view of the neat, sprawling backyard. The door that adjoined the kitchen swung open and Carla came in with a big tray of condiments.

They took their places. Steak and potatoes for Marvin and his father; a big salad for Mom.

Marvin wondered how he would eat. The last thing he wanted was food in his stomach. His father rolled up his

174

sleeves and loosened his tie. His mother took a sip from a tall glass of Tab. His father hunkered over his plate and set about the job of eating with a weary sigh.

Marvin started cutting his meat, taking his time, watching the way the dark brown of the steak gave way to pink, then juicy red. He longed to be out of this house—he'd forgotten how miserable things could be.

His mother picked at her salad, finding little to tempt her palate. She set the fork down and sighed, then looked up at Marvin with a brave but pitiful smile.

Marvin looked at the piece of steak on his fork. He opened his mouth but couldn't make the fork move upward. No way. Not in a million years.

He put it down. I'm not going to ask them for help, he suddenly thought. I'm just going to say good-bye and leave. No, I'm not even going to say good-bye. I'm just going to get up and get the hell out of this miserable place.

"What'sa matter, Marv?" His father's jaw worked busily as he sawed off another piece of steak. "Free food not good enough for you?"

"Dad," he said, and felt his throat choking up. He did not plan his next words, and was astonished at what came out. "Dad, how come you never loved me?"

Mr. Moy stopped cutting immediately. His watery eyes were enormous behind the thick lenses. "Huh? *What?*"

Marvin could feel the tears now, welling up from his eyes and spilling onto his cheeks, feeling like boiling water. "Why haven't you ever loved me, Dad? Why haven't you ever . . ."

"Why haven't I ever *loved* you!" Henry Moy gave a harsh bark. "Jesus *Christ*! You really wanna know why? You really wanna hear about it?"

"Henry . . ." Mrs. Moy's tone was one of urgent caution.

Mr. Moy began getting out of his chair, staring at Marvin

175

with a look that seemed to be fueled by the inside of a blast furnace. "You wanna hear it, kid? You want me to tell you the *real* fucking story?"

"Henry!" Cloris Moy's hands were tight on the arms of the chair, her knuckles white.

Mr. Moy put his hands on the table and leaned forward. "I'll tell you why I never liked you! I'll give it to you right between the eyes!"

"*Henry!*" She got to her feet so fast the chair clattered to the floor.

"You're *not my kid*, Marvin! You hear that? *You're not my fucking kid!*"

"No!" Cloris grabbed her husband's arm and tore at his sleeve. *"No, it's not true, it's not true!!"*

He kept his wife at arm's length, grinning at Marvin with ghastly intensity. "That's right, Marv old boy! Your dear sweet mother always liked to keep a little action going on when I was out of town, and plenty of it! Shit, *she* doesn't even know who the fuck your real father is any more than *I* do!"

Marvin stared open-mouthed. He started getting out of his chair, not knowing that he was doing so. He couldn't believe what was happening before his eyes; it was as incredible as the end of the universe.

"You ain't *mine*, Marvin! You hear me? *You ain't mine!*"

Mrs. Moy tried to claw at her husband's mouth, but he shoved her so hard she tripped and sprawled to the floor. She grunted painfully, then put her face in her hands and started shrieking with anguish.

Marvin went to her instinctively, and Henry grabbed at his sleeve. Marvin twisted away and turned to face the man, coldly certain that if he didn't back off, he would kill him. The look in Henry Moy's eyes changed from anger to astonishment. He backed away, surprised.

Marvin knelt by his mother and took her by the shoulders, gently helping her up. "Are you all right? Are you hurt?"

"Please don't . . ." She let herself be lifted, but she looked away, face obscured by her tousled hair. "Please let me alone."

"Mother, if he's done anything to you, I swear . . ."

She was upright now, but sagging against the wall. She pushed at his hands weakly. "Just let me alone, will you?"

"Mother . . . what he said doesn't matter—"

"I said get away!" She shoved his hands away with sudden strength, then glared at him with a hatred that was intensely pure. "Get away from me, you." Her eyes were narrow and evil-looking, and her lips were drawn back in a snarl. "All my life you've been nothing but a misery to me. Do you hear? A *misery!*"

Marvin stepped back, stunned.

"Get out of my house, do you hear? Get out of my house, you little *bastard*."

Marvin felt as if a great hole had opened up in the ground, that the house was creaking and breaking and falling apart all around him. This was it, he thought, the end of the world, there was no sure footing anywhere. . . . He staggered backward, hands clapped to his head, certain that his skull would surely fly apart . . . indeed it felt as if there was some kind of machine inside his head that had gone crazily out of control, and parts were already flying off the overwrought mechanism.

Henry Moy advanced, splotched hands balled up in tight fists, eyes glinting triumphantly behind the heavy lenses. "You heard her! Get out! Get the hell out and never come back!"

Marvin turned and began staggering toward the big double doors. He heard Henry Moy's footsteps, hurrying to

177

catch up. Marvin found the knob and pulled the door wide. He ran outside, hands once again clamped to his head.

"Get the hell out!" Henry had stopped in the doorway and was shouting loud enough for the entire neighborhood to hear. "Never come back! You hear me! Never!"

Marvin made it to the low hedges at the end of the property. He caught his ankle in the sharp leaves and twigs and sprawled flat. He pushed himself upright, glancing back one last time.

Henry Moy was a stout little silhouette in the doorway, shaking his fist. "Never come back, you bastard! You hear me! *Never!*"

Marvin got up and made it to the sidewalk. He didn't care where he was going; he started down the steep grade in a wide, loose gait, hands still pressed tight to his skull, feeling for all the world like a Tin Man whose bolts and rivets were popping off with each uncoordinated step.

□
S E V E N T E E N

It was only when Marvin came upon a commercially zoned intersection that he knew he was no longer in Mission Hills. He looked around, noticing that he'd managed to wander for the better part of an hour without being aware of the thick fog. Tiny water droplets swirled in a streetlamp's cone of light.

There was a small frame building, its neon VIDEO CITY sign blurred by the mist. A spanking-new Union 76 station sat close by the northbound entrance to the interstate. He saw a bus coming down the street, moving slowly as it negotiated the downgrade, its big headlights haloed by the fog. There was a stop nearby, and he felt his pocket for change. The big GM chuffed to a stop, rocking gently on its shocks, and Marvin opened his palm and saw that he had enough quarters for a ticket.

The fluorescents inside were harsh, and he was examined with little interest by the few passengers. He found a seat and leaned his head against the coolness of the window. It rattled uncomfortably when the bus started up, then settled into a buzzing vibration that was as soothing as Magic Fingers. Huge parking lots and discount stores whisked by outside, their outlines vague and unreal.

He closed his eyes. His exhaustion was complete, but the scene in his parents' house would not go away. It replayed itself like a film caught in an endless loop, full of grotesque slow-motion images of his mother falling to the floor in a loose-boned heap, his father advancing on him with great, goggling eyes.

Don't you despise them?

Marvin frowned and put his hand to his temple.

He longed to return to Kathryn's apartment. He wanted to take a long, hot shower and be held by the only person in the world who gave a damn whether he lived or died. And tomorrow he would talk with her and sort it out as best he could. Now wasn't the time, not—

Don't you despise them with all your heart?

—when there was so much turmoil and confusion making him feel like a pack mule swaying under a load of fifty-pound sacks.

Don't you hate them you hate them you hate you hate you hate—

The pain behind his eyes was excruciating. He lowered his head to his knees, moaning, willing it to stop. But it only kept repeating itself, as if keeping time to the beating of a raven's black wing—an enormous raven, cawing triumphantly.

I HATE THEM I HATE THEM I—

It was the bus driver who had revived him. Or at least shaken him back into consciousness, all the while barking *you okay, man? You sick? Don't fucking die on me, man.* Marvin had looked up at the black man without comprehension, his entire consciousness idiotically focused on the strange greenish sheen the overhead fluorescents gave the man's coffee-colored skin. He helped Marvin up, asking him if he wanted an ambulance or something, his tone not unkind. But Marvin had only shaken his head as he climbed off the bus, stepping into the mist-cooled night as if he were trying to remember how to walk.

Marvin stood at the intersection, conscious of nothing more than the sound of the bus fading into the damp night. He began walking, hands in pockets, face as slack and lifeless as a corpse's.

He thought about Kathryn, but it brought him no joy. A little while ago he had wanted nothing more than to be in her arms, comforted. But what comfort would there be when he told her his troubles? That wouldn't make them go away. They would only hang in the air, unresolved, noxious. And Kathryn wouldn't hold a man who wasn't a man at all, just an incompetent, victimized *boy*.

He stepped into the alley that ran in back of the Cota Arms. It was as dark as he'd ever seen it, and the fog made all the landmarks misty and surreal. But he recognized the spot where he used to park his old Datsun . . . and wondered what it would be like if the clock could be turned back and Dell was just now coming down from having trashed his apartment, how he'd like to give that big son of a bitch the surprise of his life, how he'd like to wrap his hands around his throat and squeeze tighter and tighter and then start banging his head on the concrete until it became all loose and wobbly and began to feel like a bag of wet sand—

But I already fixed old Dell's wagon, but good—

Marvin clenched his teeth as he went underneath the trellis of the bougainvillea and into the darkness of the Cota Arms' yard. He was so full of rage he wasn't even conscious of walking; he felt possessed by a terrible energy, making him light on his feet, as if he were almost floating. But the shrubbery he walked through was real enough, and he walked slowly, pushing branches aside, feeling his way through the stand of eucalyptus, breaking through into the clear. . . .

And the house lay before him, sharp and distinct now that the fog had lifted. It was pale and ghostly in the moonlight, and the big backyard pool was black and still.

He walked toward the mansion slowly, letting the memories of the day wash over him afresh, making his fists tighten at his side. His brain felt like a dark, rumbling cloud, boiling and churning. Abruptly, a jagged lightening bolt of a thought slashed across his mind:

I HATE THEM I HATE THEM I HATE—!!!

A gust of wind blew through the trees. He walked forward relentlessly, head lowered, his eyes tiny slits. He picked up a rock. Every dog has its day, he told himself grimly, and now that day had come.

He went to the side of the garage and smacked the rock against a small window. Glass tinkled to the floor. He reached in, undid the latch, and pushed open the window. Brushed shards off the sill. Hoisted himself inside.

Musty smell of oil, slight tang of gasoline. The Mercedes and the Continental sat quietly in their bays. Tools hung from the wall like so much butchered meat.

He began feeling the tools, knowing what he was looking for. He smiled as he recalled what that cunt had said about meeting with his family. *I'm sure they're just as eager as you to bury the hatchet.*

He felt its long, smooth handle and lifted it from its hook. The axehead was unexpectedly heavy, and it dropped down quickly. But he caught it just in time, holding it with both hands, like the way they'd shown him how to hold a rifle at port arms.

Yes, he told himself. He would bury the old hatchet.

He advanced on the door that led to the laundry room. He raised the axe on high and brought it down with a mighty smash. It buried to its haft, and he grunted as he worked it free. He brought it down again, and the door bucked in a few inches.

The burglar alarm kicked in, sounding like the period bell in a high school.

The noise angered Marvin all the more, and he swung the axe repeatedly, face contorted with rage, eyes bright in their tight slits. The door splintered apart and he kicked the jagged shards aside. He stepped through, axe held at the ready, the sound of the burglar alarm much louder now.

He ran through to the dining room, knocking the door aside so that it hit the wall with a loud bang. He ran into the hallway and saw that there was a light still on in the TV room, a glowing from that big damn TV set, and a silhouette frozen in the doorway, and in the background he heard Henry Moy upstairs, shouting *Who's that? Who's there? I got a fucking gun, you hear me! I got a fucking gun!*

It began deep within his gut, working its way up like a stagnant air bubble in a marsh.

Marvin screamed, straining his lungs with the effort. It filled the night, reverberating off nearby houses, and as it trailed off he sank to his knees. But the straining was far from done. His mind burned with an urgent, metronomic command:

STOP IT STOP IT STOP IT STOP

Harsh light was suddenly thrown over him and Marvin looked up, disoriented. It was the single flood that covered the backyard of the Cota Arms. He saw the black outline of Kathryn on the back porch.

"Marvin? Marvin? Is that you?" She began running down the steps. "Marvin! What is it?"

They drove in silence. Kathryn negotiated the turns grimly, embroiled in her own thoughts. Tonight you humor him, she told herself, but tomorrow you're taking him straight down to the county mental health clinic. However nice he is most of the time, there's something about him that's definitely not right.

She glanced at his profile. He was sitting stiffly upright, nervously rubbing his hands between his legs, acting as if he were getting ready to burst.

She recalled how he had raved about his parents nearly being murdered, clutching at her arm, telling her to call the police right away. Breakdown, Kathryn thought. He's having some kind of mental breakdown. Something terrible must've happened when he went to see them.

But of course . . . she hadn't felt so odd calling the police this time. And right away. Not after the other times that he'd—

She gripped the wheel hard. Maybe it was all just nothing. The Moys could've just left the answering machine on, not wanting any late night calls.

But as they neared the Moy's neighborhood Kathryn began to sense that something was dreadfully amiss. Red-

and-blue police lights flickered off the neighboring homes. A *lot* of them.

"Oh my God," Kathryn said, surprised that it came out aloud. She glanced at Marvin. He was sitting rigidly still, eyes wide and staring.

She pulled the car to a stop half a block away—there were too many cars around to hope for a parking space closer. They got out and, without thinking, took each others' hands as they went up the sidewalk. A police helicopter flew low overhead, momentarily deafening.

There were more and more people as they neared the house. Neighbors, mostly—some in bathrobes, others in hastily donned jogging sweats and pullovers. The talk among them was a loud, constant buzz, full of questions.

Their approach was finally blocked by a tall policeman. "Just keep it back there, folks."

"I know those people in that house," Marvin said. "I'm their son."

The cop gave him a quick, appraising look, then lifted his arm as if it were a gate. "All right. That guy over there with the bar on his collar is Lieutenant Colquin. Go see him and identify yourselves."

Kathryn and Marvin both went through. A TV news cameraman was taping the scene, his floodlights throwing huge shadows against the house. Two prowl cars were parked in the driveway. The rear double doors of an ambulance were being slammed close.

"Oh, my God," Kathryn repeated. "Oh, dear sweet Jesus."

Marvin scanned the scene briefly. He looked at the man identified as Lieutenant Colquin, who had a flat, no-non-sense face and a dark brush cut. He was talking to a man, a woman, and a boy, all of them dressed in pajamas and robes. They were standing close together, arms around each other, and the boy—a tall, gangling teenager with buck teeth—was staring at the cop and talking rapidly. Colquin kept nodding as he wrote in a pocket notebook.

Marvin tightened his grip on Kathryn's hand. They began walking toward the cop, and as they got closer they picked up what the boy was saying.

". . . and when I turned off the TV to go to bed I heard this crashing sound, like a limb from a tree had fallen off or something, and I looked out my window over at the Moy's place and it was just then that I heard some lady, I guess it was Mrs. Moy, screaming her head off so loud I could feel the hairs on the back of my neck start to stand up and then the screaming stopped, real sudden, just like that, and I heard a man shouting, sounded like Mr. Moy, and I couldn't hear what he was shouting but then I heard a noise like firecrackers going off, I guess it was pistol shots, and then Mr. Moy's shouting turned to screaming and it went on for a long time, the sound coming and going like he was being chased through different parts of the house and I tell you, it was really gross, and then the screaming stopped all of a sudden, like the first time, and then I saw that my dad was at my side and looking out the window and he told me he'd already called the police and . . ."

□

E I G H T E E N

A dozen people were gathered around the opened graves, listening to the Lutheran minister read the committal. He was young but enormously dignified, and his words carried easily on the stiff breeze. He kept his thumbs tight against the flapping pages of the small Bible. Two bronze-colored caskets lay in their racks, ready to be trestled down.

Kathryn tightened her grip on Marvin's hand. It had been three days since the murder, and nothing, absolutely nothing, had been sorted out. Time had taken on a strange stop-start quality, making parts of it roar along like a Blue Angels fly-by while others were curiously frozen, like a prehistoric insect caught in amber. Such as now, standing in the bright sun, looking at these hideous coffins. She knew that the more she wanted the service to hurry up, the more it would be like the pot that never boils. But whenever she tried to think of something else, her mind kept wandering back to that stupid "Twilight Zone" she'd seen the other night.

It was on one of the UHF channels, sandwiched between two late-late movies. Marvin was asleep. She watched the familiar opening sequence with little interest, taking idle hits off an almost-gone joint, and then the story had come on. It was the proverbial dark and stormy night. These people, this man and this woman, were waiting in a deserted bus station somewhere. The woman was distraught—she kept catching glimpses of someone who looked exactly like herself. . . .

Kathryn felt her skin crawl as she stared at the little black-and-white. She told herself she should switch channels, but she remained frozen to her chair, watching it all. Listened to the woman say that there were doubles out there, that they were trying to take over. And then the man—Martin Milner, of "Route 66" and "Adam Twelve" fame—saw his double leaving the bus station. He chased after it, yelling for it to stop, but the other Martin Milner only ran faster, smiling this terrible little smile as his arms and legs pumped high, glancing back over its shoulder and actually *smirking*. . . .

Kathryn leaned against Marvin's shoulder. If this service kept on much longer she knew her knees would buckle and she'd go down in a loose-boned heap. She retightened the grip on his hand and laced her fingers through his forearm. And kept thinking of that last shot of Martin Milner, staring wildly into the night, the camera closing in on a face that was terrorized and baffled all at once . . .

Marvin hardly noticed Kathryn's sagging weight. His eyes kept flickering over to his sister's marker—right next door, so to speak—and he swallowed thickly.

All day yesterday had been spent with a lawyer by the name of Lew Hubert. He'd worked with Henry Moy for years, and had even set up Henry's first corporation. Mr. Hubert bore a strong resemblance to Casey Stengel, except for being more rough and craggy-looking. His appearance was not at all mitigated by his somber, beautifully tailored suit. He had good news and bad. He got to the bad part first.

Old Henry, Mr. Hubert explained, was one of those people who always put off making their will, as if writing it up would put them under some kind of jinx. So everything was going to be probated by the state of California. Their bite was going to be thirty-five percent, and that, Lew said sadly, was right off the top, before anyone else could shoulder their way up to the trough. And there were quite a few parties already standing in line, taking numbers like it was Saturday afternoon at Baskin-Robbins.

"Your daddy had his hands in quite a few pies," Mr. Hubert said. "Nothing too big on its own, but Henry liked to think the whole was greater than the sum of the parts, if you see what I mean. A lot of moving things around, shifting capital from this place to that, lots of turmoil. My specialty is estate planning, and it got to be kind of painful to work with old Henry these last few years."

Mr. Hubert put on his reading glasses and consulted the first of many files. Marvin knew his father had been a minority partner in a Buick dealership and a full partner in a furniture warehouse, but Mr. Hubert listed two more car dealerships that were news, and then something called Moy

Development, which held options on several parcels of land near Del Mar. And that was just the major stuff. Marvin couldn't follow it all.

Mr. Hubert finally took off his reading glasses. "Pretty complicated. Worst case, which is what I'm figuring on, is that everything gets liquidated and then divvied up amongst the claimants. And, son, I'm sorry to say the house has to go into the kitty, too."

Marvin nodded. He didn't give a damn about the house.

"So to put it all in one nut," Mr. Hubert said, twirling his reading glasses, "your daddy was worth better than five million dollars, at least on paper. You're going to get a hell of a lot less than that, son. A *hell* of a lot less." He put the glasses back on and peered at a worksheet in one of the newer files. "I did some rough figuring, and after everybody gets their fill you should wind up with six hundred and twenty-eight thousand dollars, approximately." He took off the glasses and looked at Marvin sadly. "I wish it could've been more, son. I wish Henry had let me set things up better."

Marvin stared at the lawyer stupidly. Mr. Hubert got up and extended his hand. "You can stay in the house until it's sold, of course. Just check with me if there's anything in particular you want to keep. Stay in touch, and if you need anything, let me know."

Marvin stared at the bronze caskets, wondering when he would start feeling good about all that money. It meant a whole new world for him, a fresh start, everything. But his insides remained stubbornly cold and empty, and he kept telling himself that the nightmare would only end when the killer was finally caught, that it was really imperative that justice be served, that the guilt he felt . . . that the guilt he felt . . . was just . . . what anyone would feel in a situation like this. Sure it was. He had to look at it as if . . .

as if his parents had been killed in a car accident. He would've felt the same guilt; anyone would, after a horrendous argument like that. It was stupid to assume any kind of responsibility for what had happened.

He ran his hand over his mouth. If the service went on much longer, he was going to vomit. But there was a sudden chorus of mumbled *amens*, and a communal stir as people began to move away from the gravesite. Kathryn tugged at Marvin's elbow, but he remained fixated, staring at the coffins as if entranced.

"It's over, darling." Now that it was over she felt full of a manic, reedy energy. And a desperation to get out of this place. "Let's go."

He moved awkwardly, tearing his eyes away reluctantly. Kathryn took a firm grip on his elbow, guiding him uphill to the parking area.

"Like to get some lunch?" Kathryn asked.

"No thanks, Liz."

"*Liz?* Marvin, what are you—"

"Oh, I . . ." He shut his eyes and shook his head. "Just thinking about my sister. Kathryn, I'd just as soon go back to my parents' house and change, if you don't mind."

"Of course." Kathryn had driven Marvin to the big house earlier that morning to pick up something to wear for the service. He had found a dark Robert Hall number from his high school days in a corner of the basement. The jacket was tight across the shoulders, and the pants barely covered his ankles.

"Feeling okay, Marvin?"

"Fine. Nice service."

"Yes, it was just lovely." She opened the Volvo's door and started to help him in as if he were an old man. "Sure you're okay?"

Marvin was just about to buckle his seat belt when he

froze, staring at something past Kathryn's hip. She turned and looked.

There was a man in the distance, standing by a solitary oak.

"What's the matter?" she asked.

"How . . . how long has that guy been there?"

"Him? I think I saw him when the service first began. Just some creep who gets his jollies watching funerals, that's all."

She closed the door, went around to her side, and got in. Then she started up the car and got moving, anxious to get away.

Marvin sank lower in his seat, wondering why it was that Sergeant Perry found this funeral so interesting.

Marvin became increasingly restless and uneasy as they approached his parents' house, and by the time Kathryn turned into the curved driveway, he was ready to tell her to head straight to Ocean Beach. But the engine was off before he knew it, and he couldn't think of any logical reason to turn back.

Kathryn pulled the parking brake up. "All ashore who's going ashore."

His smile was so forced it was ghastly. "Yeah, home again, home again, jiggedy jig."

"Is something wrong?" She put the back of her hand against his forehead. "You really don't look very well."

He shied away, opening the door. " 'S okay, really. Let's get this over with."

Kathryn got out and joined him, taking his arm as they went up the walkway. "Over with?"

"Let's just say this place doesn't hold a lot of happy memories for me."

"I know, darling. I know." She drew herself closer. "It's too bad. This is such a beautiful home."

Marvin looked at its white bulk and grimaced. Tree shadows shifted across the walls and windows, moving slightly in the afternoon breeze. It was strange, but it was almost as if he were already inside, observing his own approach. He took the key the lawyer had given him and handed it to Kathryn. "Here, you do the honors."

She smiled brightly as she worked the lock. "*Après vous, monsieur*."

Marvin entered, eyes wide, certain something was amiss. He scanned the living room and looked down the hallway toward the kitchen. All was still and quiet, but it was a strange sort of quiet, like the inside of a department store after closing time . . . and now under patrol by roving dobermans.

"Did you hear me, Marvin?"

"Huh?"

"I was asking if you were going to inherit this house."

"Uh, no. The lawyer said it was going to have to be sold to pay off some debts."

Her face fell. "Oh."

Marvin started walking toward the kitchen, and Kathryn fell into step. "That's a shame. I thought you might—"

"Live here? Forget it."

"Well, sell it or something. Anyway, I guess it doesn't matter. Debts, huh?"

"Yeah. Mr. Hubert explained it. All my father's assests will be sold, and I get whatever's left over."

"Did the lawyer say . . . how much?"

"Something over six hundred."

"Just six hundred dollars? Gee."

"No. Six hundred thousand."

It took a moment to sink in, and when it did Kathryn grabbed his elbow. "Did you say six hundred *thousand*?"

"Yeah, that's right."

"Jesus Christ, Marvin. Are you *kidding*?"

"No." He turned and continued on his way. Kathryn watched him go, too stupefied to do anything but sit heavily in one of the hallway chairs, where she stared into space fixedly.

Marvin entered the kitchen. His clothes were in the breakfast nook, where he had changed. The basement door was still open, and he went over to close it, telling himself there was no need to go down *there* anymore. Just as the lock caught he thought he heard something. He turned around quickly and caught something out of the corner of his eye, a blurred shape that seemed to wisp out of sight before . . .

But it was only the sheers on the French doors that led out into the garden, gently billowing . . . from the gust created when he had closed the basement door, of course. He took off his jacket as he went over to the sun-filled breakfast nook. He undressed quickly, anxious to get back in his beach clothes and out of the house.

"Marvin?"

He nearly jumped. "Wha—what?"

Kathryn walked into the kitchen slowly. "Six *hundred* thousand dollars. I just can't get over it."

"What about it?"

"What do you mean, 'What about it?' My God, Marvin, this is going to change our lives."

He almost yelled *What do you mean OUR* but caught himself in time, surprised at the anger that had suddenly flared up. "Let's just get out of here, Kathryn. We can talk later."

He peeled off his underpants, feeling the same sort of self-consciousness he'd experienced in a high school locker room.

194

Kathryn touched his shoulder. "Hey."

"Hey what?"

Her voice was low, with a faint contralto of nervousness. "This is crazy, but . . . would you believe I'm . . ." She looked perplexed yet determined. "Marvin, would you like to make love?"

He was about to put on his cutoffs, but he slowly straightened up. Kathryn was near enough so that he could feel her body heat. She'd worn black for the funeral, but it was a dance outfit, the skirt long and demure, but with an attached top that was so tight and low-cut she'd worn a dark shawl. Which was now in the Volvo. Kathryn leaned close, putting her arm around Marvin's neck, pressing herself against him so that a warmth kindled in his belly and slowly flowed downward like sweet molasses.

"How 'bout it, big fella?" she whispered. "Right here. Right now."

As close and easy as a glass of water, but Marvin found himself holding back. Something was wrong in the sweetness, something corrupt . . . after all, she *was* his sister . . . even though . . . it would be so easy . . . so very easy, to sink with her to the floor, peeling her out of that top and having it out right there, hammering against her warm abundance with all the savagery he could muster. . . .

"No," he said breathlessly. He took her arm from his neck. "Not here, Liz. Let's just get out of here and go home."

She stepped back unsteadily, her eyes so glossed over that she seemed drugged. "What's . . . darling, what is it?"

Marvin stepped into his shorts and snapped them on, pulled on the tattered UCSD sweatshirt. He picked up his tennis shoes, deciding there was time enough to put them on later. "C'mon."

He took her hand and led the way from the kitchen, not knowing why there was a sudden imperative to leave the house as quickly as possible. But the urgency only grew stronger as he neared the front door, and by the time they were halfway down the hall he was fairly dragging her. He had a sudden urge to turn around and look behind him, but he resisted it, tightening the grip on her hand and opening the front door and pulling her out into the afternoon, where there was only the sound of the breeze whispering through the tall eucalyptus.

"My . . ." Kathryn looked confused, as if she didn't recognize her surroundings. She ran her hand through her hair, pulling it away from her face. "Marvin . . . ?"

"Give me your keys. I'll drive back to the beach."

"Marvin, I feel so . . . I—"

He wrapped his arms around her tightly. "I love you, Kathryn. I love you more than anything in the world. Remember that always."

She put her arms around him, still dazed, but his warmth felt so good. "Darling, darling, darling . . ."

"Come on, darling. Wake up."

Marvin groaned and rolled over. Kathryn was sitting at the edge of the futon, radiant, beautiful, dazzling in her multicolored exercise outfit. "Come on, sleepyhead. I've cooked up a big breakfast for you."

He sat up slowly, smiling. Kathryn realized with a start that he looked different than he had recently—no circles under the eyes, no lines bracketing the mouth.

"Hey, you look nice." He ran a hand through his hair. "Funny, even though I drank all that wine last night, I don't have a headache."

"You shouldn't, not after all that sleep. It's almost four o'clock in the afternoon."

"*Four?*"

"Come on." She took his hand. "Up, up, up. I've already had one of my classes today, and I feel ready to take on the world. Let's go."

He sat down to a no-nonsense breakfast of ham and eggs, and was surprised at the ferociousness of his appetite. He shoveled the food in rapidly, and when Kathryn offered to scramble up another batch of eggs, he nodded.

When he was finally done, he sat back from the coffee table feeling hugely contented, ready for anything. Kathryn was leaning on the table, head propped with one hand, beaming at Marvin.

"Listen," he began, "about yesterday . . . I know I sounded kind of funny about the money and everything, but I was—"

"That's all right, Marvin. I understand."

"—just, you know, upset. The funeral and all, and going back to the house . . . ."

She looked away. "Let's not talk about that place, shall we?"

"Sure. Yeah. Anyway, I haven't had time to really even think about what I should, you know, do . . . and how it's going to affect us."

She took his hand. "It's going to make things perfect."

"Think so?"

"Marvin, it really didn't become clear until I was giving my class today, but when it did I just wanted to start singing like a bird. I've thought it all out, and . . . well, let me just say one word to you."

"What's that?"

Kathryn's eyes were bright and intent. "Mexico."

"Mexico?"

"Yes. You've been there before, haven't you?"

"Sure, to Tijuana."

197

She screwed up her nose. "Ugh, that hole doesn't count. Places like that make everyone think the whole country is nothing but burned-out desert and run-down whorehouses. But the real Mexico isn't like that at all." She tightened her grip on his hand. "It's the most beautiful country in the world, Marvin. Honest to God. There are places there that are so lush and rich you'd swear you were on another planet. And the beaches . . . so long and white and pure that you want to cry looking at them. And you can fly along the coast for hours without seeing any condos or hotels or shopping centers or any of that crap. Just the occasional village . . . and these secluded villas where rich people live."

The words began spilling out rapidly, and the pressure on Marvin's hand became uncomfortable. "We could get one of those villas, Marvin. Shit, we could *build* one, set it up exactly the way we want. You could put your inheritance in one of those money markets and we could live off the interest, easy. Think of it. Just you and me living by an empty beach, no one and no thing to bother us ever again. You could work on your paintings all day, and I could finally have my garden. It'd be such a perfect life. Fresh fish and vegetables for dinner, then maybe a walk into the village for a drink at the local cantina. What do you say, big fella? What do you think?"

He smiled. "I think . . . I think I ought to call that lawyer and find out exactly how long it'll be before I can get my money."

Her eyes positively glittered. "Oh, Marvin."

"And then ask him about those money markets."

She scooted over and leaned her head against his shoulder. "Darling, darling, darling . . ."

"I think I have one of his cards in my wallet. I'll just give him a call now."

"Okay, fine." She glanced at her wristwatch. "Oh, hell. I have two classes tonight; I'd better start getting ready." She gave him a quick kiss and got up. "You know where the phone is."

Kathryn went to the bathroom, singing lightly under her breath. She thrummed with happy energy; surely enough, she thought, to conduct back-to-back aerobics classes all the way to midnight and even unto dawn, hallelujah. She pinned up her hair and washed her face vigorously, confident that hers was a future wherein wash basins would always be clean and sparkling new, easily replaced when the porcelain showed its first hairline crack.

She patted the towel against her face, telling herself that now, at last, the great change was at hand. The morning view of telephone poles and rooftops would be magically transformed into that of an isolated palm-fringed beach. And the person she cared about most in the world would be there to share it.

She looked at the mirror. *Everything's going to come out right after all, thank God thank God thank God.*

She finished in the bathroom and went out. She heard Marvin replace the receiver on the old rotary-dial phone. He stood up slowly, shoulders sagging.

Kathryn's stomach went cold. Bad news of some sort. She bit her lip and told herself that it had been too good to be true. She knew it all along. Just *knew* it.

She walked over to him. "Marvin?"

"Hmm, what?"

"Did you talk with the lawyer?"

He smiled, but it was more a contraction of his cheek muscles than a real smile. "Yeah, got ahold of him right away. He was real nice."

"And?"

"And, well, it seems like it's going to be several months before the estate is probated."

Kathryn thought it over. Was that so bad? "Is that all he said?"

"Oh, no. He can go ahead and give me some money now. Five thousand dollars, in fact."

"Oh, Marvin, you had me worried!" She threw her arms around his shoulders and smiled up at him. "That's plenty of money for now. Why . . . we could drive down to Ensenada tomorrow and rent some place at the beach. Get the feel of how we want things. And believe me, five thousand dollars will go a hell of a long way down there."

But Marvin did not join in on the happy relief, and Kathryn felt the chill return to her belly. He took her arms from his shoulder and sat down on the sofa. "Yeah. I kind of thought of that myself. So I decided to go ahead and check out with the police."

"The police?"

"Yeah." That same caricature of a smile came and went. "There's this officer that investigated that thing I told you about. You know, about those people who were attacked at UCSD."

"But . . . I thought that was some kind of misunderstanding. I mean, you were somewhere else when it happened. Anyway, isn't it over with?"

"It's still an active investigation, made all the more active by that thing with the gas station, and then of course my parents."

"But you didn't have anything to do with those!"

"That's what the detective said, too." Again, that ghost of a smile. "But he still doesn't want me leaving town. Not for down south. Not even for anywhere north, for that matter." He began rubbing his hands together, and a dark look passed over his face. "He wants me here."

Kathryn sat next to him. "Listen . . . it's not that bad. Surely all that will be cleared up soon, and then we can go. Maybe you should call that lawyer and ask his advice. Please don't be upset."

"I'm not upset." A muscle near his jaw bunched, then loosened. "Really, Kathryn. You just go on to your class."

"Only if you're okay . . ."

"I'm *fine*." He looked at her and grinned—or perhaps it would be more accurate to say that he merely bared his teeth—and Kathryn smiled woodenly, telling herself that it really wasn't such an awful setback, that Marvin was just taking it too hard and the lawyer would soon get everything untangled.

"Okay, Marvin . . ." She got up from the sofa and grabbed her designer gym bag. "I'll be back by nine. Take care of yourself."

□

N I N E T E E N

Sergeant Perry recradled the phone.

Mexico?

It didn't really mean a whole lot, not by itself. Even when it was factored into the rest of the equation. . . .

One of the lucite buttons at the base of his telephone began blinking.

Jack, Perry thought. It didn't mean jack.

He punched the button and picked up the phone, then tried not to sound disappointed when he recognized the raspy Brooklynese of one of his more long-winded anonymous informants, someone he'd long ago dubbed Secret Agent X-39. And X-39 had some really hot dope, worth fifty bucks easy, Sarge, and Perry sat there while X-39 rambled on and, true to form, began to spread his wampum for free. It had something to do with the Suwakabi murder, a drive-by shooting in which leads were precious few. Perry silently took notes on a yellow legal pad. It was a little background information on neighborhood gangs, worth maybe five bucks if old X-39 really got serious about asking for it, which he hardly ever did.

Then Perry felt the hairs on the back of his neck prickle, a danger signal that had been developed and honed on his first beat. He turned around quickly, the buzzing voice on the phone utterly forgotten, fully prepared to roll to the floor and come up on elbows with Smith & Wesson poised.

Nothing seemed amiss. The four-man cubicle was empty, and his view of the main bullpen did not reveal any black-hooded terrorists swarming through the office, Mac-10s ablaze.

Still . . . something seemed dreadfully awry, and Sergeant Perry strained his eyes and ears to try and pick up the stranger in the sea of familiar faces, the wrong sound in the background din of high-speed printers and telephones.

But everything . . . seemed . . . okay . . .

He returned to the yellow pad and put the receiver back to his ear. X-39 was in the middle of a pissed-off tirade, wanting to know if Perry wanted the goddamn information or not.

Perry quietly told him to fuck off, then hung up.

The detective made himself a drink as soon as he got home, a big one, easy on the Coke, heavy on the Bacardi.

It'd been a bastard of a day, and there was no home-cooked din-din to boot. His wife was at that stupid computer class at SDSU, studying Pascal or Mescal or some such horseshit.

He finished the first drink while still in the kitchen, then made himself another. He took out a Le Menu dinner from the freezer—fancified whipped potatoes and mystery meat—and put it in the microwave. He walked into the living room of the small condo and tossed his jacket on the sofa, then unlatched the sliding glass door to the balcony and stepped outside.

The condominium development was set on a hill, affording all units a spectacular view of Mission Valley. Tonight it was even clear enough to pick out ships' lights in the Pacific, some ten miles distant. It was a view that always drew the Perrys' guests to the balcony, gasping in admiration . . . and causing more than one nervous twitter at the dizzying two-hundred-foot drop to the dusty sagebrush below.

But tonight the view did not offer the momentary oblivion that Perry had come to expect. Instead he found himself preoccupied by other images, floating through his mind with lazy persistence. Like the charred remains of Mr. Sam Hattstaedt and Dell Ready, laid out at the morgue like piles of burnt hamburger. Or the way Bill Snyder had leaned over his desk and said *Thought there's something you oughta know about this double-murder up in Mission Hills—you're old pal's come up again*. Or of a haggard young girl in her hospital room, pointing and screaming as if it was the end of the world. . . .

He let the images roll through his mind, moving like billiard balls whispering over felt, gently rebounding against the cushions, clicking against other balls . . . but always, always, set in motion by one particular cue.

Perry frowned and took another pull at his drink. *Eight*

ball was more like it. Marvin Moy wasn't your typical murder suspect. He wasn't even your typical *jay*walking suspect.

Still . . .

Perry thought about the Chiplowe case, one of his first as a full-fledged detective. Bobby Chiplowe was kind of like Marvin—as nice a lad as you'd ever want to meet. Short hair, blue eyes, chinos from Nordstrom's. A preacher's boy home for the summer from Berkeley, where he was studying mechanical engineering. His girlfriend had been the captain of the drill team at SDSU. Hikers found her body up in the wilds of Mt. Palomar, bloated and dead a week, stuffed behind some bushes.

Smooth as cream was old Bobby Chiplowe, wide eyes registering shock and innocence. He held up good for two solid days, until they got the positive match between the tracks at the murder scene and the Adidas jammed in the back of his locker at the Family Fitness Center. His All-American face kept that same freshly scrubbed look, and his baby blues were as innocent as ever, but he hiked himself closer to the tape recorder's microphone and said that he had loved her, he really and truly did, but you've just got to understand what it's like to go steady with a girl for all those years, keeping yourself pure for marriage, and then find out that she's been seeing other guys behind your back, that in fact she hasn't been so lily-white herself. . . .

And Anton Perry had sat quietly, his face a stone mask, as Bobby Chiplowe told how he smashed in her skull with a rock, then hid her body in the bushes . . . and how he'd found himself drawn back to the scene night after night, drawing the bushes from the hiding place, taking off his clothes as he once again approached the corpse . . .

Perry took another slug from his drink. The night was cool but far from unpleasant, the temperature indistinguish-

205

able as either summer or winter. Jack Murphy Stadium—four miles distant and square in the middle of his view—was dark tonight, its huge parking lot empty. On Padre game nights it was really something else, bright as a piece of the sun, the roar of the crowd reverberating off the hills like the communal scream of a great prehistoric tribe.

How to go about it, Sergeant Perry wondered. In a case like this there weren't many options. Get Marvin someplace by himself, even an interrogation room, and . . . well, there didn't have to be any physical violence, not when there were so many other methods that were tried and true. Bill Favor was especially good at that sort of thing. And for a creampuff like Marvin, it wouldn't take too long to bust the lock open and see what goodies were inside.

He finished his drink. It wouldn't be nice, and Marvin would never be quite the same after Bill Favor had his way, but . . . Perry set his mouth grimly. What had to be just plain had to be.

Then he felt the skin on his neck draw as tight as a brand-new snare drum. He got up quickly and turned around, part of his mind thankful that he still had the .38 in its little clip holster at the small of his back. He knew with cold certainty that someone was in the condo, and the Smith & Wesson was in his hand before he consciously willed himself to draw.

But there was nothing; not even so much as a darting silhouette or a fleeting shadow. Nothing but—

Perry didn't think it was real at first. Been working too hard, he thought. Or maybe it's just that I need glasses after all. He squeezed his eyes tight and passed a hand over his face, but when he opened them again the thing was still there, stupifying in its strangeness, actually becoming more real.

It was shapeless, dark, and transparent. It hung over the

sofa, roiling like a small, angry thundercloud. And, as Perry watched, the thing actually began to coalesce and take form, with vague outlines of arm-shapes and leg-shapes.

Perry's terror increased like a steel band drawn tight around his chest, squeezing the breath from his lungs, making his eyes bulge from their sockets, and he felt that if he could only scream there might be some release, that the thing happening before his eyes would disappear.

But he was frozen, unable to run, unable to scream, barely conscious of the prickling sweat that sprang from every pore. He watched the thing start to take on a grotesque man-shape, twisting and straining as if trapped inside an invisible net. The face began to take on form, features crystalizing into a portrait of agony. . . .

Or was it anger? Perry thought crazily, and he saw that the legs were making running motions, but since there was no purchase for them it looked like the bicycling motions a child might make when jumping feet first off a high dive.

Then the creature suddenly became whole, and all trace of the cloud disappeared as the man-thing drifted to the carpet and finally found its purchase and there was nothing slow-motion about it anymore, it was barreling at Perry as fast as a bolt of lightning, and Perry fired point-blank, the sound like a cannon in the small living room, but the thing kept up its relentless charge and line-drived into Perry, slamming him against the balcony's railing, and Perry felt the creature's terrible solidity and warmth, and he held onto it desperately as the world turned upside-down and he went backward over the railing and felt the cool night air turn into a roaring wind and the lights of the valley and the condominium complex cartwheeled around him with fantastic speed.

□

T W E N T Y

Marvin decided to do at least one constructive thing while Kathryn was gone, and that was to clean up the kitchen.

But time got away from him in an odd sort of way, making the chore seem strangely fractured and disjointed, like a patchwork quilt with half the sections gone.

He pulled his hands from the cold water of the dishpan, and they were pruned and wrinkled. He stared at them stupidly, trying to make sense of it. One moment the water's hot and frothy with suds, the next—

—the next he's smack in the middle of an unfamiliar living room, looking at a person standing on some kind of a terrace or balcony, and he turns around and it's Sergeant Perry, eyes big as silver dollars, and he pulls out his pistol and—

A savage migraine flared up just behind his eyes, making his knees buckle. He sagged against the counter, grimacing, damp hands pressed against his temples. He desperately wanted to scream, but the only sound that came out of his mouth was a raspy hiss. He sank to his knees, blinded by the terrible pain, certain that if he could only scream there would be some kind of release—

—just as Sergeant Perry was finding his own release in a great death-scream as he dropped through the night like a stone, arms and legs working crazily—

—and Marvin fell to his side, balling up on the cold linoleum like a fetus, telling himself that everything was going to be all right, that the pain would go away any minute, that someone would reach down and draw him out of this bottomless well of pain . . .

—as indeed there was, leaning over the ledge and reaching down, calling for Marvin to grab onto his hand and be pulled up into sweetness and light and sanity, and Marvin gratefully put his hand into the strong grip and was pulled up quickly and effortlessly, and then he was face-to-face with his benefactor and though the sweetness and light was truly abundant there seemed to be a definite shortfall in the sanity department, yes, sir, things weren't quite up to snuff there, matter of fact it made you want to forget about screaming and go ahead and laugh your head off until your hair was gray and the heavy-duty straitjacket had turned into rotten canvas, the sound of your laughter loud enough to echo down the tile corridors and drown out the gibbering hoots of the other inmates because, after all, you're carrying a heavier load than anyone else in the bughouse and you've got a right, man, an absolute right to all the giggles you can muster when you're car-

209

rying murder on your mind, and not just plain old everyday murder like for Sergeant Perry and Mr. Sam and Dell Ready and Professor Willings, gosh no, that was weak lemonade compared to what you really had to think about, killing your own—

Marvin got to his feet, steadying himself against the counter. He had no idea how long he'd been out, but at least Kathryn wasn't back yet.

And he knew that Sergeant Perry was just as dead as a stone.

Marvin pushed his hair back from his forehead. He had seen it all, just as if he had willed himself into that apartment and—

What? Did the things that were done to his parents, to Mr. Sam, Dell, and that professor?

But . . . he hadn't really wanted those things to happen. It had just sort of gotten out of control. . . .

What's gotten out of control?

Marvin took down a plastic tumbler from the cabinet. His hand shook as he filled it with water. *It* had done it, he told himself. *It* was something he couldn't control. He really wasn't responsible for—

Trembling, he checked his wallet and saw there was enough cash. He went into the living room and looked up the number in the phone book, then called for a cab. He left a message for Kathryn on a yellow Post-it note: *Gone home.*

TWENTY-ONE

Marvin stared at the house a long time. The moonlight gave the white paint a strange luminescence, and the facade was ribboned by the shadows of the tall eucalyptus. The house seemed alive and dead at the same time, like a corpse infested with parasitic life.

He'd felt all right during the ride in the cab. Full of grim determination, even an eagerness to get on with it. But as soon as the cab pulled up the curving driveway, his insides had begun to feel like a bale of loose straw.

He took a deep breath and started going up the walkway,

conscious of each step as if he were trying out a pair of stilts. This was the domain of . . . whatever. This was where it somehow drew its power, and daily it became stronger, until finally . . .

He had to find it, talk with, *see* it—something!

Marvin took the key from his pocket and slid it in the lock. He felt the pin-tumblers click into place, and he turned the latch. He touched the door and it swung open noiselessly. His mouth felt as dry as a cottonball.

He stepped inside. None of the curtains was drawn, and the moonlight cast bright rectangles on the floor, filling the interior with a silvery half-light. Marvin strained to detect any movement, any sound. But there was only a certain heaviness to the air, something almost electrical—and quite enough to make the hairs on his forearms stand lightly on end.

He was about to say something—wasn't sure what, he just wanted to announce his presence—when he heard a muffled *thump*. Marvin swung his head toward the noise. There was another thump, followed by a barely audible shuffling, and Marvin stepped forward, looking to see what it was.

He took a deep breath, and the air that went into his mouth was as thick and heavy as the steam from a teakettle. "Okay," he said, and the word came out hoarsely. He cleared his throat. "Okay. Here I am." He stared, wide-eyed, waiting. *"Here I am!"*

The last came out much louder than he'd intended, and it startled him. He waited for the noise to die away.

There was a slow, slithering sound, and then a bump. Followed by a barely audible moan.

Sweat prickled Marvin's scalp. The noise was coming from upstairs . . . and the last thing he wanted to do was go deeper into this house. Matter of fact, it was downright maddening when he thought about how cool and fresh the outside air was, how easy it would be to turn around, go out the front door and keep walking, head off into the neighborhood and lose himself in the night, breathing deeply and thinking of . . . nothing, nothing, nothing.

But he made himself move forward. His legs felt heavy and thick, and he went toward the staircase slowly, like a statue trying to come to life.

There was another bump, a quick moan. He gripped the banister firmly, pulling himself up, concentrating on the effort of bringing each leaden foot to the next riser. The sound became louder . . . and more rhythmic. The back of his shirt was damp.

He reached the second floor, and the noise seemed to be coming from down the hall where his old room was. There was a woman's moan now, a moan that made the hairs on the back of Marvin's neck prickle, and then a grotesque sound of masculine passion, like the snort and snuffle of a pig. Then the rapid bumpety-bump of something hitting the wall.

He stood in front of his room, where indeed the noise was loudest. His hand shook as he reached for the door, but he pushed it open.

It swung only a few feet before it smacked against something just inside the doorway—a rounded, black shape balled up on the floor.

Marvin stepped back. He saw that it was a man—kneeling, weeping into his hands. The snorting sound wasn't coming from him, but—

The man looked up slowly. The mortician's heavy pancake makeup was streaked and clotted. There were slashes on his face where the coroner had roughly pasted things together with thick surgical string, and the broken skull made his face as lumpy as a piece of rotten fruit.

213

Henry Moy slowly got up, holding onto the door for support, staring at Marvin with eyes that were dusty and dead. He was trying to say something, although this was difficult for someone whose jaw had been pulverized by an axe. He reached out beseechingly, and the door swung wide, and then Marvin saw what it was that was making the grunting and banging, it was coming from the pair on the long sewing table, a couple engaged in a grotesque parody of lovemaking, rutting amidst the fabric bolts and tissue-thin dress patterns and overturned Singer. His mother was on her hands and knees, the dress in which she had been interred roughly pushed up over her waist, and the thing that slammed itself against the loose flesh of her buttocks was just as he feared it would be, a perfect replica, exact in every detail, its face contorted with a strange mixture of savage anger and triumph. . . .

Marvin ran.

He cried as he sprinted down the hallway, all courage gone, and he grabbed onto the banister and swung himself around and began going down, taking the risers four at a time, but it was strange how they seemed to stretch out like an accordian, becoming longer as he speeded up, now curving and spiraling down upon themselves like something out of a Dr. Seuss drawing, a nightmare staircase with paintings on the wall shaped like huge parallelograms, showing him moving pictures as he hurried down; Sergeant Perry falling through the sky, arms and legs thrashing frantically; Genevieve Collier in her hospital bed, posing as if she were a humid centerfold, connected to a battery of medical equipment by a score of tubes and wires; a slow-motion clip showing an endless replay of Mr. Sam pressed between a gas pump and a motorcycle's handlebars, his body slowly splitting and rupturing—

He made it to the bottom of the stairs and started running

214

through the house. The hallway was as long as a football field, and the walls stretched up into infinity. He ran on, desperate, rushing by chairs that were so tall it would have taken a ladder to climb to the seat, and then the big TV set was suddenly before him, awesomely gigantic, its screen grown to drive-in proportions, and on it was the flickering image of his mother, the colors lurid and wavering; her hands lifting up to ward off the blow, hands that could no more fend off the sharpened blade than they could stop a falling safe, and the silvery edge slammed into the fingers of her right hand, pushing them back against her face as the blade smashed in and buried itself to its haft—

Marvin screamed, shutting his eyes tight and falling to his knees.

T W E N T Y - T W O

Kathryn found the note on the refrigerator, and she kept re-reading the message as if the two words were hieroglyphs from a Tibetan monestary.

She found her way to the sofa and sat down heavily. All through the exercise class she'd known something was wrong, and she'd tried her best to put it from her mind. She'd thrown herself into the quickening tempo of the music, really giving her students their money's worth, and they'd followed her lead obediently, the long mirrors on the wall making it seem as if she were manipulating hundreds of women in jarringly bright leotards. But even as she'd led her class through the rigors of knee lifts and side kicks, she couldn't shake the notion that the dam was crumbling and everyone should get the hell out of town.

Kathryn bit her thumbnail, staring at the coffee table. She wondered what bothered her more—Marvin's absence, or . . . where he'd gone. There was something about that place that was horrible and unsavory. You could stand in the kitchen's sunlight and feel chilled to the bone. And the other rooms, with their surprising warmth, offered no comfort, only a sensation that made your skin crawl with revulsion.

She thought about the peculiar way she'd acted in the kitchen. Lord, had she ever wanted to make love more desperately? If indeed that was the appropriate expression. More like she'd wanted her brains screwed out, right on the floor if need be. And had there been a dozen men lined up behind Marvin, that would've been fine, too.

But the desire had been extinguished as soon as she walked out the door. . . .

What on earth could he be doing back there?

She got up and began pacing, thinking about the way Marvin had looked when the police told him to stay in town, that strange mixture of helplessness and anger.

She took a glass from the cabinet and opened the refrigerator. She poured the wine, telling herself to just wait it out . . . and to ignore the chill that had slowly gathered round her heart.

Marvin brought his breathing under control. He took his hands from his eyes and looked into the darkness, and the black shapes of furniture and paintings were . . . back to their correct size, at least. He felt relief, but it was a cautious sort of relief—the kind someone feels when they come to a level part of a rollercoaster ride. Marvin got up slowly—surprised at how much effort it took; he felt as tired as if he'd run a marathon—senses as sharp and alert as he could manage. It was utterly quiet, utterly still. And the aura of malevolence had completely dissipated, making the house seem rather like

a power cell

drained of its charge. Marvin became sure that if he were to go back upstairs he wouldn't find . . .

"It was just a trick," he whispered. "Nothing but a trick."

He saw that he was in his father's study. A big rectangle of moonlight covered the slate top of the teak desk. The far wall was dotted with dark shapes of various sizes—plaques and certificates from a grateful Chamber of Commerce. The door to the hallway was open, and he could see all the way down to the front entrance.

Marvin walked over to the big desk, which was covered with an untidy pile of papers and file folders. He picked up a letter and examined it in the moonlight. Moy Development letterhead, with a cryptic note to an unfamiliar real estate broker. He looked at the other papers, and they seemed equally insignificant, but there was a coldness in his chest when he wondered who might have left things in such disarray—it had been clean yesterday.

It might be gone, Marvin thought with a small flicker of optimism. Perhaps it had overexpended itself with the

illusions? You really think they're illusions?

Marvin tilted his head quizzically. The words had come softly, but they'd been spoken nonetheless. He looked to the right and above, where the sound seemed to have come from, but there was nothing there, only the darkened corner of the built-in bookcase. He wiped his mouth with the back of his hand, thinking that it wasn't over yet. Not by a long shot. There was something about this house that still had a certain

power, yes, power, let's call it power because power's what it's all about—

"Where are you!" Marvin wheeled in the darkness, staring, listening. It was deathly quiet, really an unusual sort of quiet, the kind that's

so . . . fucking . . . quiet . . . it's . . . like . . . a . . .

Marvin's eyes were drawn to something in the hallway, something that was vaguely defined, something that even gave off a soft phosphorescence . . . which seemed to increase in intensity even as Marvin watched, making the breath in his lungs go as cold and dead as the dark side of the moon. The thing was about the size of a basketball, hovering a few feet in the air . . . floating toward the study . . .

Fear welled up quickly, threatening to seize total control, but Marvin found enough nerve to force himself to remain steady, preparing himself to face whatever this new illusion was. And that's all it was, Marvin told himself, just another illusion, something that wasn't—

—What? Real? You'd better fucking believe it's real, unless of course you'd like SOMETHING THAT'S REALLY FUCKING LOUD—

The words banged in his head like brass cymbals, and Marvin put his hands to his ears, squeezing his eyes tight and groaning. Exhaustion swept over him in a sudden wave, and he started to double over the desk. He thrust his hands on the slate and stopped himself, knuckles turning white as he strained to push himself back up, telling himself it was very important that he remain standing, ready to face whatever it was that was coming down the hall, and when he looked up he saw the glowing thing was already in the study's doorway, and it was no longer a ball-shape but more like a man-shape—

—You don't know how often I tried to help you—

—growing and taking on ever greater definition even as its phosphorescence dimmed, and Marvin strained to remain standing, fighting the overwhelming urge to give up and sprawl backward in the big leather judge's chair—

—You don't know how often I tried to bring us together and make us whole so that life could be lived as it should. But no. Whenever I tried to take you with me, whenever I tried to bridge the gap . . . why, you were too chicken to even get *laid*—

He stared at a thing that was no longer hazy and undefined—the glowing was almost gone, leaving something that looked like the image from a dusty antique mirror. Marvin licked his lips with a dry tongue. "I never needed you—"

—I'd say you've got that one backwards—

"No, I never wanted . . . whatever it is that you had to give—"

—Come on—you never wanted Genevieve?

"Genevieve, I . . . I may have wanted her, but—"

You'd have spent your whole life mooning over her IF I HADN'T DONE SOMETHING ABOUT IT!

The words stabbed between his eyes, making his knees buckle. But Marvin held tightly to the corners of the desk, steadying himself, and he brought his eyes up to face it again. "I may have wanted Genevieve," he whispered, "but I never wanted . . . to harm anyone . . ."

YOU NEVER WANTED ANYTHING SO BAD, YOU GODDAMN HYPOCRITE!

The words exploded like a string of cherry bombs, but he managed to hold himself upright, tears of effort trickling from his tightly closed eyes. "You're not real." It came out between clenched teeth, like a hiss. "Go away. I command it, I *order* it—"

It stopped near the front of the desk, the grin leaving its face. Marvin thought he saw some uncertainty there, but the moment passed and the smile was back, sudden as a magician's trick.

—Well now, what's this? A fight? Don't you think it's a little late in the game for that when you've spent your whole life being pushed around?

"You're wrong. All my life I've been trying to become what I really—"

—What a load of—

"—am, to find out what sort of person I truly—"

—You spent your whole fucking life DENYING what you are—

"I always tried to live as best as I knew how, even though Mom and Dad kept trying to—"

—You were just as much to blame as they, don't you see? YOU were just as afraid of what was underneath as dear old—

"No, that's not true, not true at all—"

You ALL wanted to keep me down, keep me from living MY life—

"It was *never* your life, goddamn you, *never* your—"

Oh, BABY! Now that's where you're DEAD WRONG—

"*I'm* real and you're not!" Marvin pounded his fist against the desk, glaring fearlessly. "That's what matters—and there isn't a thing you can say or do to change—"

WRONG WRONG YOU COULDN'T BE MORE WRONG *I'M* THE REAL ONE I'VE *ALWAYS* BEEN THE

REAL ONE THIS IS *MY* BODY NOW DO YOU HEAR THIS IS *MY* BODY YOU'RE THE TRESPASSER NOW DO YOU HEAR ME YOU'RE THE TRESPASSER—

Marvin cried out, scarcely feeling the desk's sharp corner as he went down. He clapped his hands to his ears as he rolled on the floor, telling himself that if he only kept up his own yelling he could keep it out of his mind—

But things had suddenly become quiet. Marvin looked up and saw the thing was very near, almost standing over him, looking down and smiling. It was complete now, every detail defined, its strange luminescence gone. Marvin took his hands away from his ears . . . and stared at them in horror. His hands had begun to take on their own soft glow. . . .

The words came again, quietly, without menace:

I don't know how long it's going to take. I don't even know where it is you'll be going to. Maybe into nothingness. Maybe into the attic, or your old room, who knows? Wherever it is that ghosts go, because that's all you really are. That's all you've ever been . . .

Marvin looked up. The thing still smiled, lips unmoving:

. . . but perhaps you'll be around long enough to watch me go back to Kate's apartment, which is a little piece of business I've been meaning to attend to.

Marvin grabbed the edge of the desk and started to pull himself up, straining as if he were lifting himself over a rocky outcropping of the Matterhorn. He was angry, and the anger seemed to give him strength. . . .

You know, that Mexico idea isn't half bad. Of course, Acapulco's more my style, and it sure as hell isn't anything I want to do for more than a few weeks . . . but I guess the length of our stay is entirely up to Kate.

Marvin felt as if there were no bones in his hands, that they would slip free at any moment. He grimaced and pulled

222

and let himself think about the thing being with Kathryn, and Marvin finally pulled himself shakily upright.

The party can go on so long as things are interesting. And then . . . well, there's supposed to be Mexicans who'll actually *buy* women, you know? Americans supposedly get the best price. 'Course, I'd have to dye her hair blond, but . . .

"No, goddamn you!" Marvin gripped the desk hard, using his arms to shuffle himself near the thing, wanting nothing more in the world than to fling himself upon it. *"You're not getting out of here without a fight! You're not—"*

FORGET IT, BOY! IT'S ALREADY OVER, YOU'VE LOST, YOU—

Marvin cried and gasped at the pain, but the pounding inside his head evaporated as suddenly as it had come, leaving a complete silence—except for a new noise, one that wasn't inside his head . . . and Marvin looked up—past the thing's shoulder, where the thing itself was looking—and saw movement in the hallway. The big front door had swung wide . . .

. . . and Kathryn stepped in, a small silhouette bathed in moonlight.

"Marvin?" Her voice sounded distant, strange and underwatery. "Marvin? Are you here?"

Well, my oh my . . .

The words again resounded as if from the center of Marvin's head. And echoed from the figure standing before him after a millisecond's delay. It had spoken. The thing looked back at Marvin and gave him a sly little grin.

Looks like the fun begins a little early, eh? You'll have to excuse me now.

It strolled into the hallway languidly, pulling the study's door closed. Its click was barely audible. Marvin's insides clenched with nausea. The worst of all possible worlds had come true . . . and he was utterly drained, feeling as if his limbs were no stronger than newspaper.

"Marvin, are you here?" she called. "Is that you?"

He made himself move toward the door, using the desk's top to shift himself along, like a man with paralyzed legs. He knew he must follow it, knew he must find an advantage—*hadn't that languidness been too studied?*—but every passing moment seemed to decrease his strength by half. He came to the end of the desk and pushed himself toward the door—glowing hands reaching out for the knob—but his legs refused to take his weight and he sprawled to the floor. He wanted to cry out, but when he opened his mouth there was no sound.

"Oh, darling . . ." Her voice was small, relieved. "It *is* you—"

Marvin grimaced with rage and frustration, pushing himself up. His mind ran in frantic circles, like a rat cornered by a bull terrier.

"Marvin . . . ?" Relief gave way to uncertainty. "Is something wrong?"

There must be some reason why it's left me alive—there must be some reason it didn't strangle me or stomp or just kill me when it could—it can't or won't harm me: there must be something about this process that it doesn't want disturbed—

"Marvin, what are you—*oh my god!*"

Anger and desperation acted like a catalyst, giving Marvin enough power to grab the desk and pull himself up. And in that moment he thought of the gun his father always kept in the top right hand drawer, the one he always bragged he would use to punch out the clock of any shitbag burglar—

He pulled himself along the desk, feeling as insubstantial as a puff of vapor. He grabbed the drawer's handle and pulled, and god damn but didn't it feel like he was trying to pull one of those granite boulders they used to build the Pyramids—

Kathryn began screaming.

Anger goaded him, and the drawer slowly came open. The squat little automatic lay atop a sheaf of papers, glinting in the moonlight. Marvin grabbed it with a hand that was glowing brightly now—but not so brightly that he couldn't see the outline of the pistol's grip *through his damn hand* . . .

He grabbed it and relief flooded through him when he found that he could still feel its cold oiliness, but Christ Almighty when he tried to pick it up—

Kathryn's cries had become a series of shrieks, and mixed in with it was the sound of echoing laughter.

—it was like trying to pick up a jeep by its front bumper, and Marvin roared with frustration, his desperate love for the woman wrenching his insides as if his organs had exploded . . . and the pistol suddenly lifted free—

DOWN NO NO DOWN PUT IT NO DOWN NO NO YOU DAMN DOWN DAMN—

The words inside his head were sudden, deafening, nuclear. He lifted the pistol up and the study's door suddenly burst wide, the thing rushing through with its eyes wide, its hands outstretched.

DOWN DOWN PUT IT DOWN YOU DON'T YOU DARE DON'T YOU DARE NO DOWN DOWN DON'T DON'T DON'T—

The thing leapt across the desk as Marvin pressed the barrel against his skull, and he felt a final moment of savage triumph.

"NO, DON'T DO IT! NO! YOU DON'T KNOW WHAT YOU'RE DOING!"

Marvin's head jerked sideways at the force of the thunderbolt.

T W E N T Y - T H R E E

It's like being marooned on a fucking asteroid, the boy thought. Nothing to look at but a bunch of tumbleweeds and cactus, all laid out on terrain that was just about as flat and uninteresting as a dusty Ping-Pong table.

He kicked a rock and it bounced up against the gas station's office. Faded pennants fluttered in the hot breeze, making a plasticky rippling sound. He would've liked to have been inside, taking it easy, but the air conditioner was on the fritz again and the windows were swelled so tight in their frames you couldn't pry them open with a crowbar.

Someday the old man's gonna bust a gut yelling at me, then I can sell off this dump and get the fuck out of Nevada.

He sighed and started to go back into the office, deciding it was the lesser of two evils. Besides, it was time for his eighth Pepsi break of the morning. But just as he put his hand on the door something bright and shiny glittered in the distance, catching his eye. He squinted and saw that it was a car, painted some king of metallic flake, kicking up a small cloud of dust as it came down the road.

The boy leaned into the office, took the icepick off the desk and slipped it into the wrench pocket of his coveralls. He went over and stood by the lone pump island, wiping his hands with a rag, smiling his biggest smile. *Come to poppa, baby. Been a slow morning and need me some extra cash, yowzah.*

It was really barreling along and the boy thought it might pass on by, but it slowed a half-mile down the road and angled for the station. It was a brand-new Lincoln, the silver paint job marred by a battalion of splattered bugs. The boy closed his eyes when the slipstream swirled by, making the pennants sway in a hot cloud of dust.

The boy walked over to the driver's window, grinning. Blue and yellow California plates, which was usually a good sign. The tinted window rolled down, allowing a gust of frigid air to escape. The driver was a balding guy with Mr. Toughshit wraparound shades.

"Yes, sir? Fill up?"

"Premium." It came out short and clipped, but the boy knew it was an act. You could always tell these types no matter how tough they tried to act. He went over to the pump, doing secret cartwheels at the bonanza-to-be. *Prime*

California fruitcakes, couldn't have ordered up better; just the type that didn't care if the credit card slip said twenty or two hundred. He put the nozzle in and set it on automatic, got the washer and did the front windshield, then walked around to work the back. There was an old babe in the passenger seat with a nice enough rack, but hair just as white as a pitcher of milk. The only other passenger was a scrawny young snatch sitting in the backseat, wearing a hospital gown and staring at the carpet like it was the most interesting thing in the world, same expression to her eyes as those on the dried-up old lizards Bob Collins sells at his roadside stand.

The boy judged the moment carefully, then dropped to his knee and slipped the icepick from his pocket. *Looks like this old boy's going to need himself some new rubber today, yessir. And once this boat's inside the bay, why there's just no telling what all's going to be wrong under the hood. Sure as shit the carb's going to be all fucked up, might even be fun to see what the guy thinks with a couple of Alka-Seltzers sizzling away in the battery cells—*

The shadow fell across him suddenly, and the boy looked up, bowels suddenly loose and watery. Holy Moly, but did the son of a whore have a *size* to him. He had the pick up against the treads, one hand ready to smack the handle home. He tried to think up something about how he was just cleaning out the dirt when the boot came whistling up out of nowhere and caught him on the the jaw. A ragged explosion went off inside his head, and he was unaware of flying through the air and hitting the hardpacked dirt. He tried to push himself up, still thinking there was some way to talk himself out of it, but the boot whammed deep into his gut and when he cried out bits of teeth and blood came out of his mouth. The boot slammed into him again, and the Pepsis and cheese crackers came whooshing up out of his gut, and the guy lifted up his boot and the boy was only dimly aware that he was about to be stomped.

And then he was.

Three times.

It took a long time to get some air back into his lungs. He tried to push himself up, but nothing worked. Even the effort of moving his arm sent bolts of pain rocketing through his body. He opened an eye—the other was swollen shut —and was surprised to see that the Lincoln was still there.

It was like looking through the wrong end of a telescope. The man had finished gassing up and was putting the nozzle back in the pump. He flipped the lever closed and walked around the rear of the car, flashing a toothy grin at the boy. The boy immediately closed his eye, instincts telling him to play possum.

Lord God, how could you be so goddamn stupid? The boy cursed himself silently. How could you've pegged him so totally wrong?

He cradled his ribs—*Jesus K., all busted up inside*—and wondered where he'd read the clues wrong. Everything had pointed to easy pickings. He wondered how long it would take to crawl back in the office and call his dad. And what kind of story he could tell Sheriff Brammer that would get this bastard locked up for a hundred years.

The Lincoln's engine roared to life and the boy opened his eye. The big car started backing up, building up speed, and the boy felt his broken insides go as cold as ice water as the left rear tire grew bigger and bigger and bigger . . .